FALLING STAR

FALLING STAR

RED WITH NATIVE BLOOD

BOOK TWO

MARJORIE CARTER

RANDAL NERHUS

SOUL MISSION PUBLICATIONS

Red With Native Blood: Book Two: Falling Star

Copyright © 2022 by Randal Nerhus

For inquiries contact: www.randalnerhus.com

This is a work of fiction. References to real people, places, or events (historical or otherwise), are fictitious in nature. Names, characters, events, and places are products of the authors' imaginations. No resemblance to actual places, persons (living or dead), or events is entirely coincidental.

Library of Congress Cataloging-in-Publication. Data is available on file.

ISBN: 9780998717531

Page design by Caryn Pine.

Cover design by Getcovers.

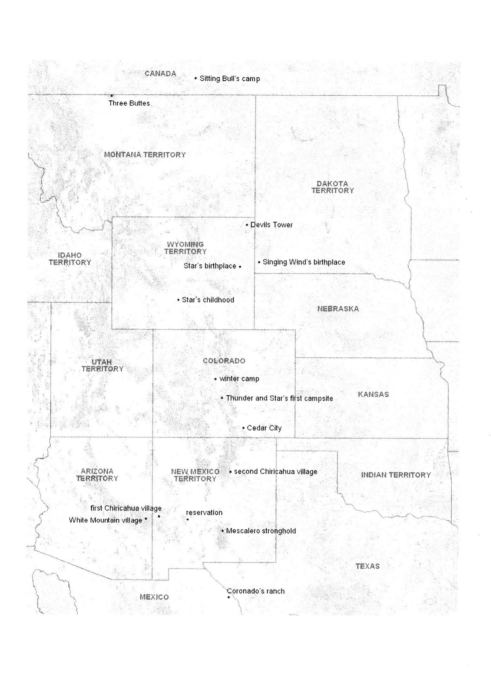

FALLING STAR

Far from one-year-old Desert Flower, then living in the White Mountains, something happened in a millisecond on the Great Northern Plains. An ancient soul returned to earth from the spirit world to serve the Cheyenne people by planting the seed for a tribal rebirth.

ONE

Dakota Territory
(present-day Wyoming), July 1865

The village was quiet. Children, adults, and old ones sat by the communal fire, sipping tea after the evening meal. Father Sun had gone to rest, and murky clouds blocked most of Moon Maiden's reddish-orange light as she slowly rose above the horizon.

"Look, everyone, look at the sky!" Red Flower screeched. All eyes followed her gnarled finger to an eerie cluster of dark clouds above them.

The full moon appeared through an opening in the eastern clouds, most of it blotted out, only a remnant shining. The world bathed in unearthly light. An unexpected chill embraced the village, a vicious wind whipping across the scorched earth.

"Death stalks our village this night!" another woman wailed, as a coyote howled from somewhere in the nearby mountains, informing the shaman that evil spirits were loose in the night.

Great streaks of lightning veined the sky and a clap of thunder jarred the earth. Rain spattered in huge drops, blending into a solid wall of water. Villagers ran in haste for shelter. Abruptly, the rain stopped and the moon turned an ugly, dark blood red.

"The storm gods have eaten the Moon Maiden!" came a distressed cry from the darkness.

"Quiet, old woman," Red Flower grumbled, "or they will eat us too."

Suddenly, for one breathtaking moment, a star arced its way down toward the earth, blazing with pure white light. The star exploded, radiating a blinding flash. The stunned villagers stood speechless, looking at one another in bewilderment.

From the birthing tipi, the cry of the shaman, Raven's Wing, shattered the silence and resounded throughout the village. The Cheyenne people, renowned for their bravery, now cringed in fear, waiting for death's blow by some demonic hand.

After some time, Long Bow and his Dog Soldiers, their weapons ready, cautiously crept toward the tipi. The coyote's warning had made them anxious to learn Raven's Wing's fate. When the warriors rounded the tattered lodge, their eyes widened in surprise, for at the entrance stood their shaman.

Raven's Wing, the most esteemed holy man in the Cheyenne nation, stood calmly rocking a newborn baby. The long tendrils of his yellowish-gray hair glowed, and the dark circles under his sunken eyes made him appear ghoulish. The awe-stricken warriors stared at the shaman as if he were an apparition from the spirit world.

Finally, Long Bow regained his senses and stepped closer. "Grandfather! We thought the demons had come for you!"

"No, my son, I have seen no demons. I cried in joy when I saw this miracle birth. My vision has come true!"

The frightened women and children still expected the worst as they crept behind the Dog Soldiers.

"Sound the drum," Raven's Wing directed. "We must call the tribe to council."

Raven's Wing's pronouncement spread through the village like a windswept fire. Moments later, the heavy thuds of the drum summoned everyone to congregate at the middle of camp. Chaos ensued as the adults sat, jostling for their favorite positions in a circle enclosing the central clearing. Everyone talked at once with no regard for customary courtesy.

"What do you suppose has happened?" Lame Leg asked.

"I do not care to guess," Spring Clover said, shrugging her bony shoulders.

"The end is coming," Red Flower declared. "The end is near."

Astonished, the women turned to Red Flower. "Why do you say that, Mother?" Lame Leg asked, even more curious than before.

"Too long we have had to run from the Wasichus, who are taking our land. Though we know our prophet Sweet Medicine warned us against following the invaders' ways, drinking their firewater alone has made us foolish. The Great Spirit has been offended, and now comes the day of reckoning. Now comes the time for our punishment."

Red Flower's words stunned the people into silence as they hunched over and crossed their arms. Their fear of the presence of spirits caused them to stay on guard for something to happen.

At last, the aged shaman appeared, looking mysterious with his face painted in black and white polka dots. He stepped through a gap in the circle of seated Cheyenne and emerged into the vacant center. Like an ancient oak, Raven's Wing represented a timeless strength. Although his fringed leggings hung loosely about his frame, their bead and feather ornaments cast a sense of elegance. His sunken chest was bare, save the yellow orb painted to resemble the sun.

A spine-tingling hush fell upon the crowd when the old man lifted his arms to the sky. The gourd rattles in his bird-like hands came alive to tell an ancient story, his worn moccasins moving gracefully to the rhythm.

The primal throbbing of unseen drums joined in, causing each heart to quicken. When the tempo reached the proper pace, the warriors joined Raven's Wing inside the holy circle. They began a summoning dance to invite the spirits of their ancestral fathers to this sacred meeting.

Raven's Wing lowered his arms, and the drumming stopped. Most of the warriors seated themselves with the people in the outer circle. Some, however, remained in the sacred area, where they stood in a new, smaller ring. The old man took his position of honor in this circle of the council. He sat cross-legged, and the others seated themselves according to their stations.

When everyone settled, Raven's Wing opened the pyramid-shaped bag of soft white deerskin and took out his long-stemmed red clay pipe. He methodically lit it and drew in smoke. The first puff he blew up toward the sky, saying, "To the home of all spirits." The second went downward. "To Mother Earth." The following puffs went to the four sacred directions:

West, to the land of thunder spirits who give us rain.
North, to the spirits who send us great cleansing
winds.
East, to the spirits of light who give men wisdom.
South, to the spirits of summer who hold the power to
grow all living things.
All these spirits are forever aspects of Maheo, the
Great Spirit, the All-Knowing One Above.

Raven's Wing passed the pipe to the warrior on his right, who did not smoke from it but handed it on to the next man. Thus, the warriors passed the pipe around the circle, unsmoked, in the direction opposite the sun's course. Upon its return to Raven's Wing, he blew smoke from the pipe and gave it to the man on his left, following the course of the sun. Each man took his turn, believing the ascending smoke to be his own breath carrying his words to the Great Spirit.

When the ritual was complete, Raven's Wing set the pipe aside to cool before returning it to his bag. He slowly rose and began to speak, despite murmurs in the crowd. "I have called the ancients to this council to verify the miracle we have witnessed here tonight. They are here to guard my tongue so no untruth shall be spoken.

"Many years ago," Raven's Wing began in his best story-telling voice, "the Great Spirit sent the prophet Sweet Medicine to teach and guide his Cheyenne children. Before Sweet Medicine died, he predicted what would come to pass in later years, including our present time. For you young ones who may not know his revelation, I will give you the gift of his wisdom."

The children and adults fell silent and turned toward Raven's Wing.

"'One day,' Sweet Medicine proclaimed, 'the time will come when you must fight, for each tribe will want the land of another. My children, you will be driven from your land and earthen lodges. You will no longer know the tranquility of life as growers but will be forced off the land and out of your dwellings. For the Cheyenne nation to survive, you must become hunters and warriors. You will be nomads and find refuge in the west, on the Great Plains. You will live in skin-covered lodges, eating the meat of a great shaggy-haired beast. With the passing of many seasons, there will come a strange animal. It will have round hooves and teeth on the top as well as the bottom of its mouth. It will have long hair growing from its neck and a hairy tail that almost drags on the ground. You must not eat this animal but learn to ride upon its back. For when the shaggy beasts grow fewer, you will have these 'long tails' to help you hunt for elk and deer.

"'When the shaggy beasts are no more, there will come a smaller animal with short hair. Some will have spots of color on their hides. The meat will not be as sweet and succulent as the shaggy one; none-theless, you must learn to eat it, or our people, the Tsetsehesestahase, will die.'"

The crowd stayed silent, and their eyes widened.

"'During this time, there will be many changes in your lives. Strange men will come from a faraway land. Their skin will be white, and many will have eyes the color of the sky. Some will have hair growing on their faces. These men will eventually rule the land. You will follow the ways of these white men and become worse than crazy.'"

Raven's Wing sank slowly to the ground, his frail body quaking from exhaustion. He was very old, so old that even the next-oldest member of the band could not remember a time when he was not already an old man. Although he had earned the respect of every chief in the Cheyenne nation, here he was more than respected—here he was loved. Many times, he had proven himself a great healer and advisor. The fact he had lived so many years was proof enough he communed with the spirits.

The Cheyenne people waited for their shaman to regain his breath.

Seeing the people face him and begin to whisper, Raven's Wing seized the chance to reclaim their rapt attention. Silence fell as he rose, took a long draught from his waterskin, and began to speak again.

"We know the words of Sweet Medicine are true!" He paused to be sure all were once again listening. "Just as he predicted, our ancient fathers were forced from their native land of the Five Great Lakes. We have indeed become hunters and warriors who roam the plains. We also live in tipis, ride horses, and hunt the disappearing buffalo. We are exactly as he proclaimed we would be.

"If we cannot go back to our traditional ways, the rest of the prophecy will come to pass. We will live on the white man's reservations, where they will strip our way of life from us. Is this not the worst fate? To lose everything we hold dear?"

Raven's Wing paused to let these truths touch each heart. "We have watched the sky-eyed strangers take our land and kill our buffalo. We can do nothing, for they are countless. Like blades of grass on the prairie, for every one we kill, ten more appear. They have already forced our sister tribe, the Southern Cheyenne, to move far south to a reservation alien to us. I do not wish to go where so many have gone and never returned. The buffalo are our food, clothing, lodging, even our tools and weapons. Without them, our people cannot live as the ancients did. As Sweet Medicine foretold, we must learn to eat the meat of these strangers' 'cattle.'"

A powerful spirit seemed to fill Raven's Wing. "The words of Sweet Medicine," he declared, "no longer hold hope for us. Another leader, another prophet, must speak to us and intercede with the spirits, that the Cheyenne may yet live under their guidance. That leader has come to us now!"

Drawing a deep breath into his shallow lungs, he gave the people another moment to absorb the truth of his words. He continued. "Many moons ago, a spirit came to me in the night, saying, 'Watch the sky, my son. You will know when the new leader is among you, for I shall light the path to earth with a star.'"

Raven's Wing gestured to Fears No One, the baby's father. He rose, cradling a blanket-swathed infant in his arms, and approached the shaman.

"Tonight, my brothers and sisters," Raven's Wing intoned, "when Moon Maiden hid her lovely face in darkness, I witnessed a star plummeting to the earth. At that exact moment, this child came howling through the tunnel of life!"

As Raven's Wing took the infant from the blanket, he gazed into the newborn's black, glimmering eyes, seeing a light, a depth of soul, that confirmed his intuition. In his arms, he held a messenger from the Other World.

He turned and lifted the squirming baby toward the crowd. "Here is our new leader!" he proudly proclaimed.

TWO

Dakota Territory
(present-day Wyoming), July 1865

"It's a girl," someone whispered.

The young warriors stared at one another, confused. However, most of the tribal elders, including war chief Long Bow, believed the phenomena proved the girl was their shaman. Certainly, Raven's Wing's endorsement answered any further doubts. Raven's Wing ended the meeting and tenderly gave the infant back to Fears No One.

As the women and children left the grounds, the younger men jeered, refusing to even consider obeying the demands of a girl. Glares and upheld fists showed their discontent.

Raven's Wing was disquieted by their rowdiness, but it didn't surprise him.

Through the early night, warriors discussed the ramifications the newborn would have for the tribe.

"We will be laughed at if we take orders from a girl," Buffalo Bull lamented.

"We will obey only powerful men," Broken Lance confirmed. "That is the way it has always been, and the way it will always be."

The warriors rushed to stand beside Broken Lance, wanting to show how many fighting men the tribe would lose if the elders persisted with this nonsense. Cheyenne men were tall and agile. They were hardy warriors and skilled hunters and held many competitive war games to keep themselves in prime mental and physical condition. To take orders from a girl was unthinkable!

The women, having fewer formal societies, later convened a meeting to discuss Raven's Wing's surprising revelation. They crowded into a large tipi on the outskirts of camp and seated themselves inside. Mother Hawk, Chief Elk Horn's wife, rapped her walking stick solidly against a big drum to quiet the chattering women. "I have called everyone here because of the baby girl who Raven's Wing believes will be our new leader. Many of the men stand against her and may keep her from maturing into a shaman. My first question to all of you," Mother Hawk said slowly as she looked pointedly around the lodge. "How many of you believe the girl born tonight is destined to become our new leader?"

Hous of affirmation resounded throughout the lodge.

Taken aback by such an enthusiastic response, Mother Hawk rapped on the drum again. "Come to order, ladies, please." She then tried the opposite approach. "Does anyone think we should *not* accept this child as our new leader?"

The entire lodge became silent. Mother Hawk called out, "This is your last chance!" No one made a sound. "Then, it is unanimous. We agree to accept her as successor to Raven's Wing."

Hous resounded throughout the lodge again. The Women's Society had never before agreed unanimously on any issue; this was an extraordinary event.

Mother Hawk hammered on the drum many times more before regaining control of the meeting. When the women quieted, she lowered her voice to a near whisper. "Since we all agree this girl will someday be our shaman, we will encourage her whenever she behaves in unusually holy or knowledgeable ways. We will teach her to see, act, and think as a shaman is normal and expected. For her sake, we must subtly and carefully do this around the men."

"Then, we should inform our husbands, should we not?" Lame Leg asked.

"For the love of spirits, no!" Red Flower yelled, even before Mother Hawk could answer.

"No," Mother Hawk concurred, "we must not tell our husbands, or the men will think we are trying to control them. Our choice to stand with the girl as our next shaman needs to go to our graves with us. Does everyone agree?"

Again, *hous* carried the motion. The women joined hands and swore an oath of secrecy.

Raven's Wing held fast to his convictions. It did not matter to him that the child was a girl. Intuitively, he knew she was destined to be the Cheyenne's next great shaman.

Although Snowbird and Fears No One disliked this intrusion into their personal lives, they honored the tribe's welfare above their own wishes. They made no objection when the old shaman named their child "Falling Star."

As the moons passed, the controversy over Falling Star's future leadership continued, but no one could deny her exceptional nature. She radiated a feeling of an ancient soul, elevated beyond the cares and concerns of ordinary people. As word of the fulfillment of Raven's Wing's prophecy spread throughout the Cheyenne nation, the women in every band supported her appointment.

Cheyenne women were among the most attractive of Plains Indian women and Falling Star's unique beauty surpassed all expectations. Her small, heart-shaped face displayed perfectly chiseled features, and her dark brown eyes shone brightly with intelligence.

Raven's Wing observed how the child bonded with her surroundings without fear of anyone or anything. His visions revealed she had not come to live a conventional life with the Cheyenne people, but rather to serve them. In the years to come, the Great Spirit would lead her to a far northern land to fulfill her destiny.

THREE

Dakota Territory
(present-day Wyoming), August 1867

The next two years further confirmed Sweet Medicine's prophecy. Lack of food and the soldiers' continual attacks upon the village pressured Chief Elk Horn into negotiating yet another truce with the general. Three Star assured Elk Horn of the Cheyenne's safety during the peace talk. The ninety-seven trusting Indians moved their tipis to the designated rendezvous, anticipating provisions offered by Bluecoats.

The women set up camp near a river, just beyond the shadows of the huge fort. There, they found the promised wagon full of food. The Cheyenne were so happy to have provisions, they invited the Bluecoats to a great celebration. To honor the officers who would attend the peace talk, Indian dancers—in their finest regalia—opened the ceremony with a traditional welcoming dance. Many of the enlisted men came to join them in their dancing. They brought refreshments, and whiskey flowed through the camp more swiftly than the water in the nearby stream. No one seemed to notice the soldiers drank sparingly or not at all.

Early the next morning, Fears No One awoke to the first scream. He lay listening, unsure of what had awakened him. When the shrill sound came again, he leaped from beneath his blanket and grabbed his rifle. "Snowbird!" he shouted, waking her immediately.

"What is it, husband?" she asked, alarmed by the panic in his voice.

"Run, woman! Take Falling Star and ru—"

Fears No One's words were cut off when a bullet lodged in his throat. Blood spattered like rain inside the tipi, landing on Snowbird and Falling Star.

Snowbird choked back shock and nausea as she struggled to gather the sleeping toddler into her arms. Her hands trembled so violently it took several stabs to cut an opening in the back of the tipi. The air had already grown thick with heavy bluish smoke that seared her lungs and stole her breath. She ran blindly, colliding with Raven's Wing in her recklessness. "I am sorry, Grandfather," she panted, taking his arm to restore his balance.

"Never mind me," he scolded. "Save the child!"

Snowbird nodded and sprinted across the meadow. "If we can just make it to the creek, my love." Those were Snowbird's last words before a bullet ripped through the back of her head and exited in the narrow space between her beautiful brown eyes. Her lifeless body pitched forward, and Falling Star flew through the air, hitting the ground with a loud thud.

Falling Star lay motionless until her breath returned, then she struggled up and walked back to Snowbird. Raven's Wing found Star begging her mother to awaken. "Come, small one," he said as he picked her up, "we must flee from the soldiers."

Hot tears streamed down Falling Star's chubby cheeks as she clung to Raven's Wing, but no sound escaped her lips. Raven's Wing felt his strength diminish as he carried her down to the river, where he found several Cheyenne women on the run. Seeing no warriors, Raven's Wing assumed they would find the men in due course. After giving Falling Star to Plant Woman, Raven's Wing rounded up the stray women, children, and old ones, then led everyone into the forested hills.

The old shaman had never expected the soldiers to trick and attack his people, but their treachery had opened his eyes. The Cheyenne would never be able to surrender enough land to satisfy them. The white men would rule everywhere, just as Sweet Medicine had foretold.

The night air already carried a sharp bite as the band of Cheyenne made camp near a creek. They endured the miserable, cold night without heat, since they could not safely make a fire.

The next morning, Raven's Wing directed the women to care for the wounded. He then asked the boys to scout and round up small animals for the cooking pots. One group of boys returned with enough meat to help the band survive another day. Later, another group herded several Army horses into camp. As the people cheered, Raven's Wing thought of how to honor the boys' coup. Lacking eagle feathers, the shaman smeared black stripes of ash under their eyes to imitate the marks of a warrior.

That afternoon, Raven's Wing ventured out from the campsite to find more food. He thought about Strong Horse, his Sioux relative by marriage and longtime friend. *His village lies somewhere to the northeast. Perhaps we will find a safe haven there.*

A soft greeting from Preying Wolf and Broken Lance, leaving cover, brought him delight. After the three foraged all they could easily carry, the warriors led Raven's Wing to their hideout.

At the camp, Raven's Wing was surprised to see seventeen surviving warriors and the Cheyenne's prized horses.

Preying Wolf smiled and said, "After the battle, we slipped back into darkness to rescue any wounded. While there, we saw some of our horses. We looked for more of them this morning. Luck must have been with us, for by midday we found them all."

Raven's Wing thanked Preying Wolf for recovering the horses, then shared his idea to find Strong Horse. Preying Wolf agreed and suggested they return to Raven's Wing's camp at once to tell their people. He called the warriors together, and they set out.

The women and children cheered when they saw the warriors approach. After the excitement faded, word of Raven's Wing's proposal spread among the people, and they made ready to depart the next morning. Raven's Wing took stock of the band, which now numbered about sixty, including fourteen uninjured warriors. They had lost forty souls in the attack, including Chief Elk Horn and Long Bow, the war chief. The survivors now looked to Raven's Wing for direction.

The shaman drafted Plant Woman, a midwife and healer, to be Falling Star's foster mother. He directed the women to care for the wounded and the warriors to scout the terrain.

The following sunrise, the shaman called his people together and performed a funeral ceremony for those who had perished. He did not bother with needless prayers, for the soldiers had already mutilated the dead. Since the people had no way to avenge their deaths, the trapped spirits would wander among the hostile whites forever. Raven's Wing dreaded condemning the spirits to this fate by leaving them behind, however, his highest duty as shaman was caring for the living.

The Cheyenne customarily inflicted wounds upon their bodies to express their grief. After the mourning ritual, Raven's Wing instructed his people not to do this. "My children, you must not mutilate yourselves as proof of your suffering. The Great Spirit is aware of your pain, and your strength will be needed if we are to overcome this evil upon us. We must go now and find a safe place to live."

The Cheyenne hid like desert rats by day and traveled by moonlight. Raven's Wing was a wise old man but not a trained war leader. Because the people loved and revered him, they expected him to lead them to safety. Drawing upon his many years of experience conferring with war chiefs, Raven's Wing hurried his people across the plains, over mountains, and through canyons, with Preying Wolf's warriors hiding their tracks.

Seven suns passed, and the weary travelers could run no more. That night, they slept hidden in a washed-out gully. The next morning, Raven's Wing decided this was a good place to rest and reorganize. After a short, informal ceremony, the people elected Preying Wolf as the new war chief. A tall, stern, broad-shouldered man, he was now the most seasoned warrior since Long Bow had passed over. Though strong-minded and quick to act, he always consulted Raven's Wing before making important decisions.

The Cheyenne did not bother to elect a peace chief; they saw no need for one.

Plant Woman and her friends collected all the available medicine plants and tended the wounded. Lame Leg and two adolescent girls cared for the children, and Spring Clover oversaw meal preparations. Supplies were sparse. They cooked every edible leaf and root the children gathered, yet no belly was full.

It was very hard to leave the country the Great Spirit had given them, but day after endless day, the small group struggled across rocky plains, fighting dysentery, whooping cough, and starvation. The hunters had a difficult time finding meat, without plundering ranches. Preying Wolf had wisely cautioned any report of missing livestock would surely alert the soldiers to their presence. The women cooked dried plums, currants, and juniper berries. For meat, they ate jackrabbits, snakes, turtles, and lizards, anything to relieve the pangs of hunger. Although the rations were meager, they kept the people alive.

Raven's Wing watched over Falling Star as a mother wolf watches her cubs. When she walked the bottoms off her moccasins, he cleaned and dressed her cut and abraded feet. In the evenings, he sang her brave heart songs to ingrain courage in her spirit.

At last, Raven's Wing found his friend, Strong Horse, and his band near the Black Hills. Though well-hidden, safe, and offering enough tipis for the newcomers, theirs was a humble, worn village, lacking abundance. Whites all around them limited the opportunity to find game.

The Sioux kindly shared their paltry winter supplies, but they had also fared badly. Many of the babies and old ones had died of consumption and the coughing disease. Still, Plant Woman took Star to her heart and did her best to keep the little one alive. Though concerned for Star's welfare, she let her freely play with the Cheyenne and Sioux toddlers.

When the Season of New Grass came, the small band of forty-five Cheyenne left the Sioux and started their own camp to the southwest. Many other fugitives like themselves joined them, swelling their numbers and their strength. Now a proud village once more, they remained hidden from the armies for a long time.

As the seasons passed, Falling Star grew straight and strong, walking with an air of confidence far beyond her years. By her sixth summer, she displayed a remarkable rapport with animals. Though avoiding other people, animals approached Star, and they instantly became her friends. Unlike the other girls, she had no interest in playing with buckskin dolls. While they built miniature tipis, Star romped through the forest. Hunters often spoke of seeing her fearlessly approach mountain cats and grizzly bears.

Late one afternoon, Raven's Wing saw Star walk up to a deer as it approached through a misty haze. The look of serenity in the animal's liquid brown eyes made Raven's Wing believe it represented the spirit of all deer. It could remain as flesh and bone or manifest as a spirit. Certainly, Star found her totem animal.

Every day, Raven's Wing told Falling Star stories from Cheyenne legend, the deeds and adventures of their forebears. He spoke of their people's two great medicine bundles, the storehouses of holy power: The Buffalo Hat and the Sacred Arrows. These brought prosperity to the tribe if correctly honored in ceremony, or misfortune if not treated respectfully. He spoke of the Creator giving the Cheyenne prophet Sweet Medicine the Sacred Arrows and told many other stories of their greatest hero.

One evening, Raven's Wing told Falling Star one of the tales of Sweet Medicine. "After our prophet knocked a Cheyenne chief unconscious during an argument, the warriors chased him in order to punish him. But every time the warriors drew near to Sweet Medicine, he vanished, then reappeared far away on the horizon."

"Teacher," Star interrupted, "people say *you* can do that. How do you do it?"

"Such powers come from the Great Spirit," Raven's Wing responded, "so be patient, little one. Perhaps one day Maheo will bless you with that gift."

Early one morning, Raven's Wing told Star of his previous night's vision. "Someday, you will find a lifelong companion plant to multiply your healing powers." When his young successor clearly understood, he nodded, happy she would welcome a valuable aide the spirits would bestow upon her.

Plant Woman loved her strange little Falling Star dearly, and, in turn, the girl accepted her as a mother. Plant Woman's sister and mother willingly shared in the responsibility of caring for Star, and they often discussed how best to raise this unique child.

One day, Star returned home with a large honeycomb and presented it to Plant Woman. It took a moment for the woman to realize the strangeness of what she saw: no bees surrounded the fresh honeycomb.

"Oh!" she exclaimed. "Did the bees sting you?"

"No," Star replied. "It is a gift from the queen bee. She told me to feed it to the sick children. She said it will help make them strong again."

Plant Woman took the honeycomb. "This is very good medicine for the sick. Thank you for bringing it to me." However, she worried about Star's safety. Meddling with dangerous creatures at her young age could be fatal. She sent her sister to invite Raven's Wing for a meal in order to speak to him about it. Later, she dosed the children with honey, as Star had suggested, and by morning, their coughing stopped.

Raven's Wing arrived at Plant Woman's lodge the following evening. When the meal was finished and the formalities complete, she brought out the remains of the honeycomb. She told him the story and of her concern for Star.

"You have no need to worry about Star's safety among our animal brothers and sisters," Raven's Wing said. "She is my responsibility when she is outside the village. I have told her this and of her limitations in the forest. I will know if she is in danger."

"If you say so," Plant Woman said, distraught. "But we have never had such an exceptional young shaman among us, and I needed your guidance. My mother, sister, and I are unsure how to raise her."

"I gave you the responsibility years ago," Raven's Wing said, "because you are a healer yourself."

"But Falling Star is unlike any other girl her age."

"Yes, her nature is different from that of others, I agree. Someone less wise than you might have raised Falling Star to feel shame for that difference, and she would have buried her spiritual nature for the rest of her life. You have no need to worry. Continue raising her as you are."

Plant Woman smiled with guarded relief.

After a moment of contemplation, Raven's Wing said, "Her way is her way, as it is written in the stars. The Great Spirit understands. We do not need to."

"I agree, Wise One but my heart is heavy. I fear what fate has in store for her."

Raven's Wing picked up the honeycomb and inspected it carefully. Recalling his visions of Falling Star, he looked at Plant Woman calmly and said, "Time reveals all mysteries."

FOUR

Wyoming Territory, July 1877

In Star's thirteenth summer, Broken Lance and his band of braves raided a wagon train and returned with a bounty. The women enthusiastically made use of the sorely-needed blankets and clothing.

Days later, Raven's Wing and many other people began to vomit and burn with fever. Star did her best, along with Plant Woman, to treat the sick. Late one night, Star was awakened by repeated calls from Sweetwater. Stepping out of her lodge, she learned Sweetwater's daughter, Butterfly Girl, was ill and had sores in her mouth. Star took them to the central campfire, now burned down to embers. From the coals' dim light, she recognized the lesions in the girl's mouth and froze in terror, *The dreaded pox!* Rapidly regaining her composure, Star calmly assured Sweetwater she would help her daughter soon and sent them home.

Star let her mind race. *This invaders' sickness is beyond any Cheyenne medicine. Healing plants, serpentine dances, shaking rattles, pounding drums—all other methods of healing—are useless against it.* At a total loss for what to do, she wanted to speak with Raven's Wing. She knew, however, she could expect no answers from the shaman in his condition.

"Please, Great Spirit," she implored, "my people will surely die without your intervention. I beg you, show me a way to combat this illness."

Preoccupied with her people's needs, Star barely noticed herself stepping slowly toward the woodpile. Thinking only of warming herself in the predawn chill, Star absentmindedly pulled out a green branch. When she tossed the limb on the dying fire, it immediately spewed forth an eye-watering blanket of dark smoke. She reflexively clamped her eyes shut, and an image flashed before her: *Ugly black smoke rose from the blankets and clothing stolen from the wagon train. Smoke billowed up from Raven's Wing, Butterfly Girl, and everyone else stricken with the pox.*

Stunned, Star backed away from the fire. Raven's Wing had told her to inform him when she had her first vision. Not knowing what to do, she closed her eyes to think, and another image came: *Ugly black smoke rose from people near anyone who had already given off smoke.*

Star wondered if Plant Woman could explain the message. She started toward her lodge, then stopped and glanced back at the fire again. Yet another vision appeared: *The black smoke spread to everyone in the village except for eight pox-scarred elders, whom the smoke did not touch.*

Star contemplated the images and wondered what had shielded

those elders from the sickness. She recalled Raven's Wing telling her the pox could only afflict people once. Those who survived it could not suffer from it again. The eight elders had lived through the pox years earlier. All the other healthy Cheyenne, though, had to leave and stay away.

Star knew no preventative measures could be started until she had Chief Preying Wolf's full support, so she went straight to his lodge. She apologized for waking him and explained what she had seen and learned. He gave no sign he accepted or rejected what she told him. However, he agreed to immediately convene a village meeting and let her speak to everyone not yet stricken with the pox.

The healthy Cheyenne gathered in a circle at the center of camp. Amid discontented mumbling from the men, Star instructed the people to seek shelter in some caves twenty bowshots upriver. "Take your healthy children and whatever things you will need," she directed. "But do not take blankets or clothes from the wagon train or any others that sick people have been using. Wash your belongings and yourselves with soapstone in the river, then go to the caves. Do not come back to this village. Start a new village there."

The women nodded in agreement, and Star was thankful for their unquestioning respect. She continued, "Anyone who has survived the pox of many years ago, please come to me."

Three pockmarked women and five men stepped forward.

"You will stay here with the sick and tend to them. Everyone else should leave for the caves now. If anyone in the caves shows signs of the pox, they should return here at once."

Star told the eight elders, "Take everything that came from the wagon train and burn it!"

The light of dawn spread across the land, as Plant Woman gathered some of her belongings and left the stricken village. The other women hastily followed.

Star asked a pox survivor, Bent Feather, to accompany her to Raven's Wing's lodge. Arriving there, she saw her mentor's emaciated body: his many years of long ceremonial dances and lack of food had taken a toll. As she gazed at him with empathy, a strange chill went through her body.

Thanking the spirits for the message and considering how to heal Raven's Wing and the others, Star steeled herself for the enormous task ahead. She required the complete cooperation of all the elders to fight the pox, and she needed her people to see and accept her strength. She began issuing orders like a war chief in battle. "Fill this bladder with water from the river," she told Rabbit Woman. "Boil it and return it to me."

The woman appeared dumbfounded but obeyed without question.

"Cover our shaman in his warmest robe," Star said to Bent Feather.

"No! His skin is too hot." He shook his head gravely. "If I cover Raven's Wing, he will surely burn to death."

"Uncle, I do not wish to disrespect you, but I must insist."

"But you will kill him!" Bent Feather replied, waving his hands.

Star looked at him sternly. "I do not fear the death of our shaman. His years are many. Would you prefer he die with a face so rotten, even wolves would shrink in horror from it?"

Star saw Bent Feather's resolve collapsing, so she pushed on. "Unless you do as I say, his death will be on your hands, and you will carry the guilt forever."

Though Bent Feather disliked taking orders from a girl, he did not want the blame for his shaman's death.

"If his teeth begin to rattle, send for me at once," Star called as she exited the lodge.

A crowd of warriors still lingered nearby, mouths agape, watching and waiting to see what the girl would do next.

Star shooed the men away waving her hands. "Go to the caves now!" she hissed. "Hurry, hurry!" Reluctantly, the men began walking upriver.

Once the warriors passed beyond Star's hearing range, several men began to grumble.

"They are burning the bounty I risked my life to get," Broken Lance protested, "and now this girl demands I leave my own home. Why should we listen to her?"

"I do not know," said Buffalo Bull. "I know she is only a child, but we all heard her say she had a vision."

"She seems to understand the sickness. She has a plan to keep us from getting the fever," Spirit Walker added. "I hope she can heal my two sick daughters."

"Well, Raven's Wing never asked us to burn our things or leave our homes," Broken Lance answered insolently.

"I mean no disrespect for Raven's Wing," Chief Preying Wolf said, "but he himself burns with the fever. If he cannot cure his own illness, how can he help the rest of us? Besides, he believes the spirits gave Falling Star special powers to save our people."

"Perhaps now we should give her the chance to reveal those powers, or the lack of them," Buffalo Bull proposed.

"Anyone who refuses to do her bidding should speak now and

take responsibility for the lives of the afflicted," Preying Wolf declared.

When no one answered, Spirit Walker stepped to the chief's side. "I stand with Preying Wolf."

Buffalo Bull followed and stood next to the chief. Seeing the unhappy faces, Preying Wolf voiced his opinion again. "What man can say she does or does not have healing powers? I have always trusted our shaman and still do. Broken Lance, you say you risked your life for your bounty. Will you risk it again to keep it? Or risk it by staying among the sick?"

Most of the group stood undecided. After a moment, Preying Wolf said, "No one but Falling Star claims to know what we must do. I admit she is peculiar, but no one can deny her deep fondness for animals, an evident sign of a shaman. I say we should follow her instructions. Would she have us destroy those things and have us move away from the ill if she was not certain they bring us the sickness?"

The men acquiesced and, recognizing Star as their only hope, decided to move to the caves and hunt to replace the destroyed food and hides.

Meanwhile, Star made a medicine broth of snakeroot, and forced each of the sick to drink as much as they could. She had the healthy elders build a large sweat lodge—four times the normal size—close to the river. She had them cut the lodge poles from cedar; no other wood would do.

After completing the lodge, some elders bathed the fevered people in the river's chilly water. When the patients grew cold, Star had them carried into the steam-filled lodge and had the flap resealed.

Others tended a roaring fire and used deer antlers to carry red-hot rocks from the fire to the pit inside the lodge. A water-pourer repeatedly splashed the stones, creating loud hisses and clouds of steam. He also tossed silver sage and sweetgrass onto the stones. The clean, sharp fragrance rising with the mist gave the sick ones new hope.

Over the next several sleeps, ten more sick came to Star, and she subjected them to the same healing regimen. Gradually, most of the sick became well again.

Two moons later, Star sent a messenger to bring the Cheyenne in the caves back to the village. Upon their return, the healthy Cheyenne found their loved ones had grown stronger. Raven's Wing and the others regained consciousness, and Star fed them meat broth and horsemint tea to build their strength. She urged them to continue taking sweat baths even after they could walk, saying, "The purification will help you heal more completely."

Star felt gratitude to the spirits for helping her lessen the power of the white man's illness. But she grieved for the twelve who died and the one who lost his sight. Certainly, her people would have many more encounters with the whites. She knew she had to find a way to avoid another outbreak, but how?

Within the passing of another moon, news of Falling Star's shamanistic skills had traversed the plains. Soon, bands from other tribes appeared, mostly Sioux, bringing people with sicknesses beyond their own ability to heal. Eager to understand their symptoms, Star rapidly learned more of the Sioux language.

While under Raven's Wing's protection, Star followed his instruction, but the lines of people needing healing still overwhelmed her. Each night, when she lay down exhausted, she felt his power renew her being, giving her more healing capacity and spiritual knowledge.

Many of the smaller bands stayed with Falling Star's people. As the weather turned cold, Star's village again grew in numbers.

January 1878

That winter brought a malady neither Star nor Raven's Wing could treat—starvation. Each morning, as more people succumbed, those behind had to cut new graves into mounds of frozen snow. Grief hung over the village as a heavy cloud. One bleak winter day, Raven's Wing and Star stood together, looking at the countless graves.

"With so little food, we cannot survive the winter," Star said.

"Fetch Preying Wolf," Raven's Wing replied. "Together we may find a way to keep our people alive."

When Star and Preying Wolf entered Raven's Wing's lodge, he offered them seats near the fire. He burned cedar chips to purify the lodge and chanted a plea for the Great Spirit's guidance. Star noticed Raven's Wing blink his eyes as if a message came to him. He said to Preying Wolf, "The Great Spirit agrees that our people will vanish from the earth if we do not find food."

"All winter, we have searched the land for game," Preying Wolf said. "Nothing is left." He picked up a piece of bark and threw it into the fire. "Even firewood to warm our lodges is scarce."

Raven's Wing nodded. "Then we have no choice. We must surrender to the soldiers."

"No!" cried Preying Wolf. "We cannot bow to them after what they have done to us!"

"I would agree," Star said calmly, suppressing her own revulsion at the idea. "But our duty is to save the children."

Preying Wolf gritted his teeth, then his eyes closed as his body slumped forward. He appeared more defeated than Star had ever seen him. "Yes, that is the only way to feed our children. We must cast aside our dignity, so that they may live and have a chance to earn their own." He softly bade Raven's Wing and Star goodbye as he left the lodge.

That night, news of the decision to surrender spread among the people, and despondency settled among them.

After three suns of travel, Preying Wolf surrendered at the Fort Laramie Agency with his seventy-six starving followers.

Accompanied by Raven's Wing, Preying Wolf met with the Indian agent to discuss the terms. The two Cheyenne asked for provisions for their people, and the agent agreed. He also ordered the Cheyenne to move seven hundred miles southeast to the Indian Territory, where many of their Southern Cheyenne relatives already lived.

Most of the people had heard stories that the reservation had bad water, little food, and strange sicknesses. They refused to go, and thus the matter rested for the day. But when the women went for their food allotments the next day, they returned empty-handed. The agency master would give them no rations until they agreed to move.

Raven's Wing made a powerful plea asking for food, if only enough for the children, and they finally struck a bargain: soldiers would escort the Cheyenne to the Indian Territory, providing rations for the journey. If the Cheyenne went south and did not like it, they could return. In order to eat, they traveled south.

FIVE

Indian Territory, March 1878

After two and one-half moons on the move, the Army led Preying Wolf's band to the Southern Cheyenne portion of the reservation. The soldiers departed, leaving the band with their horses.

The Southern Cheyenne welcomed their northern kindred with open arms and half-filled bowls of weak soup. Preying Wolf's people ate little, not wishing to add to their relatives' hunger.

Like all others on the reservation, Preying Wolf's people lived mostly at the mercy of the white man's paltry allotments. They could find no buffalo, and the whole land was overhunted, leaving it barren and meaningless. Though they admired the Southern Cheyenne for enduring the difficult life on the reservation, it was not the land given to them by the Great Spirit, and Maheo beckoned them to return home.

Three sleeps after their arrival, Preying Wolf and Spirit Walker, the new peace chief, went to the whites' headquarters. The assistant to the agent, a small man named Mr. Frederick, spoke Cheyenne and offered to translate. The Cheyenne told Frederick they wanted to return north. He took them to the office of the agent, who refused to grant their request. Preying Wolf stubbornly reminded the agent of the promise that they could return if not satisfied, but his words fell upon deaf ears.

Resigned to living in this new place, Preying Wolf and Raven's Wing decided to settle along the Cimarron River, near the Southern Cheyenne.

A few suns later, Mr. Frederick came to the Cheyenne with an unfamiliar boy. About five winters old, the youngster wore only a piece of gunnysack around his waist. Upon seeing them, Star came forward and inquired about him.

"Soldiers found this boy alone after a skirmish and brought him to me," Mr. Frederick said. "Unfortunately, no one understands him."

Star smiled. "I will care for the youngster."

Star brought the boy to her tipi and scrounged up enough scraps of material to make him clothing. She spent many days trying to communicate. The boy did not know the sign language used by the Cheyenne, but Star gradually deciphered his words. His name was Foxtail, and he belonged to the Navajo tribe. His starving people had traveled eastward hunting for many suns before the soldiers attacked them on the plains. Most of his people were killed, some fled, and he was the only captive.

Five days out of every seven, Star left Foxtail home to attend school with other children. The Southern Cheyenne students coached the newcomers in proper conduct in the classroom, and the new arrivals soon adjusted. During the three moons of classes before summer recess, Star learned the basics of arithmetic and English.

Just as the classes ended, diseases fell upon Star's people. Some became deathly ill, and many lay sick with measles and whooping cough. Star and Raven's Wing worked tirelessly, trying to cure the ailing.

Night after night, Star had visions of the plant of a thousand leaves. The beautiful images—and her strong connection to them—made it clear this plant was her promised healing companion. While searching the nearby forest and collecting herbs for the sick, she was disappointed she could not find the plant. However, she came upon an unusual find: a patch of bright red ocher clay. She had no use for ocher dye, but mindful of its rarity, she collected some.

Despite Star's and Raven's Wing's continual efforts, the Cheyenne lost fifteen souls. Each time a life was lost to the white man's diseases, Star opened her heart and prayed for the spirits to help her people avoid these plagues.

In mid-summer, when the hunters returned with a deer, Star approached Raven's Wing and asked him for the hide.

"What use do you have for it, young one?"

"Sweet Medicine's teaching will continue guiding us, but our people will also need new medicine. The Great Spirit wants me to create a new medicine bundle for them."

Raven's Wing stood in silence for a moment, then said, "I have sometimes thought Sweet Medicine's prophecy might be augmented. You shall have the hide, and you may do as you wish with it."

Star thanked the shaman and silently gave thanks to the Great Spirit for such a broadminded mentor. She walked away, knowing he would not ask further about her bundle. To reveal the bundle's contents would mean the loss of its sacred power.

Over the next several suns, Star searched the woods along the river and filled her bundle with all that it needed. Varieties of flora—for slowing blood loss and healing wounds—caught her attention. Among those, she most welcomed the sight of her companion, the plant of a thousand leaves. Thrilled, she whispered a prayer of deep gratitude. She sensed her special friend would alert her of danger if she kept it at her side. The plant's spirit would speak directly to her thoughts, warning her of illnesses, including the white man's.

She harvested this plant along with the others and put them in her bag of herbs, but the omen troubled her. *We only need these plants to stop blood loss and heal wounds after battle.* She cringed. *The spirits provide according to our needs.* She dreaded the thought of a bloody conflict ahead, but what could she do to avoid it? She prayed it would not come to pass and hoped to find a way to alter her people's fate.

Now that the bundle bore the essential medicine for her people, Star needed only to stain the deerskin. The ocher she had collected two moons earlier served perfectly. Its red color symbolized the blood of her people. Red also represented warmth, food, and home—all essential for the Cheyenne's restoration.

That evening, Star prayed to the Great Spirit, asking what she should do with the bundle. Just as she drifted toward sleep, her mind's eye expanded, and a vision appeared:

In a distant northern wilderness, a massive wall of ornately weathered stone towered above a river's bank. Through the corner of her eye, she saw an enormous deer running toward her. His auburn pelt rippled over the muscles beneath, and his antlers swayed beckoningly as he passed Star, her hair waving in the draft of his wake. He ran up an adjoining slope and disappeared behind the wall.

Star awoke reflecting on the vision, hoping to find a clue as to what it meant. She wondered what the future held for her, alone in a strange place.

Late in the summer season, the soldiers brought in three Cheyenne warriors, who wore nothing but loincloths and tattered moccasins. Preying Wolf called for a tribal meeting and took the warriors directly to the center of the village, where Star gave the three men stale bread and weak tea from their meager supply. A formal exchange of greetings and introductions followed. One of the warriors, Standing Tall, stepped up to speak. He told the people they were warriors of Cheyenne Chief White Blade's band. A half-moon ago, they were hunting far from the band when the Army ambushed them. Standing Tall went on to say that two years ago, he and his companions had fought against Long Hair, General Custer.

A confused silence fell around the meeting. The people had heard no eyewitness account of this, so Raven's Wing asked him to tell them about the battle.

"It happened two summers ago," Standing Tall began. "We met with our Sioux brothers and other friends, as we sometimes do, for our Sun Dance. Our chief knew the Oglala Sioux Chief Crazy Horse, so we camped near them on the banks of the Little Big Horn. Our tipis were pitched along the river in seven great circles. We were more than any man could count. Our horse herds were so large we feared they would eat all the grass in the surrounding area before our ceremony finished. All the great chiefs attended including Rain-in-the-Face, He-Dog, Little Shield, Big Road, Spotted Eagle, Red Bear, Gall, Crazy Horse, and Sitting Bull. Even Crawler and his Blackfoot warriors were there."

The people sat silently in awe of Standing Tall's words.

"It was a perfect day. A cool breeze wafted through the valley, and the birds were filled with song. The day started as any other until mid-morning, when someone noticed a cloud of red dust hanging over the valley. We thought it might be buffalo and grabbed weapons for a hunt. Then, from a distance, we heard a bugle singing. All at once, soldiers were upon us, bringing chaos; everyone ran in different directions. The Bluecoats had already crossed the river by the time I jumped on my horse and rode into battle. A storm of gun blasts sounded, and the sky turned black with arrows.

"After a time, a brave, hanging low on his horse's neck, rode past screaming, 'The soldiers are running! The soldiers are running!' When the shooting slowed, some warriors started yelping and blowing their eagle-bone whistles. Then Crazy Horse took us across the water into a copse of cottonwood trees where some soldiers had retreated. Our warriors were still shooting when he shouted, 'Let the Wasichu go!' We were amazed when the soldiers put their guns to their own heads and pulled the triggers. A scout said later that the Bluecoats did not understand our language and thought Crazy Horse had ordered a charge.

"Soon after the suicides, a warrior came running to tell us other

39

soldiers had retreated to a hilltop. We all rushed to the new battle-front, where Long Hair and his men were already pinned down; they had nowhere to run. Some of his Bluecoats fought bravely until death. Others took their lives too. In the end, they were all dead. It sickened me to see a man take his own life, and I hope I will never see it again."

The listeners were speechless. Raven's Wing broke the silence, saying to Preying Wolf, "We must try again to take our people home."

"I suggest you instead go to Grandmother's Land," Standing Tall said.

"The land north of the Wasichu's frontier?" Star asked.

"Yes. Grandmother, the queen of the country of England, welcomes us to her kingdom because our ancestors fought beside her ancestors many winters ago. I have heard Sitting Bull and Chief Gall already live there in peace. If you can cross the border, I am certain they will help you."

"Are there no Bluecoats in Grandmother's Land?" Star asked.

"Grandmother forbids the Army to enter her land," Standing Tall reassured her. "If you reach there, you will live as free as your fathers and grandfathers."

Star nodded in agreement. To live as her ancestors had, away from the merciless Army, struck a chord of hope in her heart. As she contemplated living in that faraway land, something of the spirit world nudged her. This Grandmother's Land, she felt clearly, bore a great significance.

Preying Wolf welcomed the Cheyenne warriors to stay and join his people, and they happily accepted.

Later that day, Preying Wolf again beseeched the agent to allow the Cheyenne to return north. But the agent met his pleas with angry denials.

The chief had been losing face with the younger men. Now they demanded he lead them back to their homeland, or they would support a new war chief. The tribal council refused to give in. One night, six of the youngest warriors slipped into the darkness, never to return.

As autumn approached, Raven's Wing realized school would soon resume. The agent would learn of the young men who had recently escaped and would undoubtedly punish those who remained. That, and the continuing hunger and illness in this southern land, convinced the shaman the people needed to depart. The Bluecoats would expect them to travel north to their homeland and would easily catch them. The same problem confronted them in going to Grandmother's Land. They needed to winter someplace where the soldiers would not look for them. Years earlier, some warriors had hunted along the Arkansas River, deep in the mountains. Raven's Wing and the other leaders agreed this rugged area would provide the best campsite for the winter.

The next new moon, Raven's Wing invited Star and Preying Wolf to his lodge. When everyone was seated, Raven's Wing announced, "We will leave the reservation tonight, after the soldiers have bedded down."

Preying Wolf agreed. "I will have the warriors play their nightly games on horseback, so the soldiers will suspect nothing."

"Could you place some warriors along our path to protect us as we leave?" Star asked.

"Yes. They will follow us as we pass them and cover our tracks. The warriors on horseback will leave at dawn and head north to divert the soldiers. Then circle back and meet with us in the suns ahead."

"Tell the people of the plan," Raven's Wing instructed, ending the meeting.

Upon returning home, Star told Foxtail to prepare for the escape. He nodded and packed his things for travel. She worried about the endeavor. If any part of the plan failed, many of her people would die, and the survivors would have to stay forever in this lifeless land.

Late that night, bearing only essentials for the journey, the Cheyenne crept from their lodges and walked out of camp. The men carried the burden of war paraphernalia, while the women bore supplies and children.

As planned, warriors on foot had gone ahead to safeguard the departure. They now waited at intervals to protect the passing women and children and erase their trail. The mounted warriors set up the charade at the compound. Some fed wood to the fires, while others rode in and out of camp, calling to one another as on any other night.

Star and Raven's Wing led their people through the darkness, helping the old and weak, vigilant to leave no stragglers behind. They hoped it would be morning before the Bluecoats would find a deserted camp and try to hunt them down.

SIX

New Mexico Territory, March 1879

The fluttering of a bird landing in a nearby bush startled Thunder and plucked her from musing about Golden Eagle. *Fifteen moons since we were last together. Will I ever see him again?*

She heard her stomach growl and realized how hungry she was. Listlessly, she ate wild turnips and onions she had gathered near the cave. Hunger satisfied, she leaned back against the wall of stone, momentarily closed her eyes, and mourned the loss of her loved ones.

Fighting grief, she looked around, seeing her tracks. *If I erase them, it is unlikely the white-eyes will find Grandfather's tomb out here, far from the village.* Slowly rising to her feet, and wincing from her self-inflicted mourning cuts, she saw the pole drag. *I must get rid of it.* After wrapping the poles tightly together with the willow branches, she rolled it over the steep bank. The bundle plunged into the stream, and she sighed as the current carried it away.

Returning to the cave, she picked up the cedar branch and swept out the tracks to the stream and around the tomb.

The past is gone, her spirit whispered. *You must concern yourself with the future now.* Thunder did not know this territory well. To survive, she must remain hidden and stay in the rugged mountains directly beyond the village.

Dragging the branch behind her, she walked toward the plateau. After a few paces, she wished to turn and look at the tomb for one final moment, but she knew she should not.

It may encourage his ghost to follow me. She had an urge to leave quickly and began trotting. *Farewell, Grandfather, until I join you in the next life.* She wondered if she had the inner strength to survive alone. In answer to her own thoughts, she clenched her resolve. *I will make Grandfather proud of me.* She dropped the branch and ran for the safety of the mountains. Air rushed through her lungs, and she began to believe the strength would come. The warm sun on her back reassured her, and she could feel the life force pulsing through her body.

Suddenly, Thunder tensed, the hackles rising on her neck and arms. She paused and closed her eyes to let her other senses take over. A strange odor assailed her, one she recognized immediately—the stink of the white-eyes.

Climbing a low-limbed tree, Thunder looked windward and saw six frontiersmen winding their horses up the bluff toward the village. She whispered her thanks to White Painted Woman for the forewarning, then watched in wretched despair as the scavengers dismounted and took clothing and sacred medicine pouches from the dead. Some even cut off ears and fingers for souvenirs.

Seized by a storm of anguish, Thunder buried her face in her hands and screamed silently. With a heavy heart, she thought of her deceased friends. Raising her unseeing eyes to the heavens, she cursed the evildoers who stole from the dead. Once again, she swore to avenge the killing of her loved ones.

As the scavengers left, Thunder looked at the corpses scattered across the plateau and groaned in pity. *Something must be done for them. But returning to the death site would be too dangerous. If the Whites came upon me there, I would be defenseless.*

Letting her lithe body slip from the tree, she hit the ground and hurried along the slope. She consoled herself that burying the dead would serve no purpose, for the bodies had already been mutilated. She could only help those poor souls find peace by taking a life for a life.

In the late afternoon, Thunder left the forest and started across a narrow gorge. The land was rock-strewn and covered with patches of prickly pears. The thick, barbed cactus thorns kept snaring her, slowing her progress, and before long, reopened her mourning wounds.

"Damnation!" she cursed in English, one of the many foul words she had learned from the girls at the school. She sat under a tree and tended to the worst wounds, hating the delay more than the pain. She sighed deeply and accepted that she had begun a very different life, all alone. "I should keep a record of my new life," she whispered to herself. She picked up a short stick and cleaned off the bark with her knife. Having thus made a time stick, she carved a notch into it for her first sun of travel.

Thunder resumed her lonely journey. Zebra-tailed lizards and coral snakes basked in the afternoon sun, making themselves easy prey for Grinning Bear's skinning knife. She decapitated the creatures, then stored them in her pack to roast after stopping for the night. As she made her long descent, squawks and trills of birds began to fill the air. She smiled. *The Moon of New Grass is near*, her spirit told her.

While the night began to close around her, Thunder climbed a slope along the gorge until it leveled off. Images of her slain people filled her mind when she almost fell into a pool hidden by a tangle of mesquite brush. Exhausted, she decided to make camp. Still leery of roving whites, she built a small fire in a shallow pit. After roasting and eating the reptiles, she went to the pool, brought up water in her cupped hands, and drank. Then she filled her waterskin.

Under the moonlight, Thunder examined the self-inflicted knife wounds on her arms. She had cut herself superficially for the most part, but some were deep enough to fester. She washed her cuts, cleaning them thoroughly. She had nothing with which to cover the wounds and could only hope they would heal naturally.

Thunder gathered large pine boughs together to create a windbreak. Using some smaller branches as a broom, she swept dried leaves on the leeward side and snuggled down for the night. Although she shivered from the chilly night air, it did not wake her. Later, however, the hooting of great horned owls immediately brought her to her feet.

"Owls!" she shrieked. The trees were full of glowing eyes. Even the bravest Apache warriors feared owl ghosts. *The unburied souls from the village—I tripped over Sunflower, took Grinning Bear's knife, and placed Little Bird beside Young Falcon. I must have got their blood on my clothing, and their spirits followed me. The others must have come with them. I set Grandfather free, but the other souls are stranded among the living—suffering, desperate, and dangerous.*

Uncaring of the cold, she plunged into the pool and chanted:

> My brother, Child of the Water,
> Please take pity on me.
> Make me invisible to the golden-eyed ghosts.
> Do not let them take me to the underworld.
> If you grant me this request,
> I will sing your praises each day,
> So all may know of your kind heart and good deed.

Shivering, Thunder repeated this chant and others while sitting on a boulder in the center of the pool. She scrubbed at the mahogany spots on her clothing, convinced the spirits had tracked her by the smell of their own blood. At the first graying of dawn, the owls departed. Thunder stepped from the frigid water and shook herself like Brother Coyote. Grabbing her rucksack, she resolutely slung it across her back and ran onward, happy to leave the dreadful camp of lost souls.

The morning haze had just burned off when Thunder reached the western bluffs of the mountains. She marveled at the lush green paradise below. A ribbon of blue-green water meandered lazily down the middle of a vast emerald valley. Beyond, snowcapped peaks jutted into a cloudless sky.

Standing perfectly still, Thunder watched an eagle soar across the endless blue, clutching a small rodent in its talons. After rounding its flight, the eagle landed on a ledge below. Thunder could hear the faint cheeping of hatchlings as their mother fed them. "It is the Season of Renewal," she whispered. "Soon, new life will sprout everywhere." Her desire to live on began to grow within.

Looking out over the countryside, she considered which way to go. Geronimo's band would be many suns of travel southwest, assuming he was still camped in the Sierra Madres in Mexico. Her mother's old village lay far north of that.

Not knowing what else to do, Thunder raised her arms to the sky and asked Ussen for guidance. Apaches rarely made requests of the Great One, and she felt a little embarrassed. Before the Bluecoats invaded, she had only prayed to thank Ussen. Lately, it seemed, she was always asking for something. Still, Ussen was all she had. Alone and frightened, she asked for a sign of where he wanted her to go.

As though answering her request, the mother eagle appeared before her, squawked once, and flew off to the north. "Thank you, Great One!" Thunder called raising her hands, palms up, into the air.

She began walking in the direction of the eagle's flight. She would have preferred to pass west, through the warmer terrain of the valley. Even in the off-season, the lower plains would provide a plentiful supply of yucca, mescal, and edible roots and nuts. Still, she had asked for and received an omen, and she was obligated to follow it.

Walking in the mountains, she managed to find some dried

winterberries still clinging to their thorny bushes. However, the farther north she walked, the colder it became. As the temperature plunged each night, Thunder realized she would need warmer clothing. Before she could make clothing, she would need to have skins. Before she could obtain skins, she had to have weapons. Besides, it would be impossible to avenge her people with near-empty hands. Having only Grinning Bear's knife, she decided to stop and prepare herself.

Searching the forest, Thunder quickly collected enough branches to make a bow and arrows. After making the bow, she hung it in her campfire's warm smoke to harden, then made a dozen arrows from good, strong mulberry wood. Lastly, she notched her time stick, as she had done every day since leaving Grandfather's tomb. Counting the notches on the stick, she marveled that she had walked for only sixteen suns. It seemed like many more.

As the bow hardened over the next three suns, Thunder stayed busy. *Busy hands are happy hands,* she recalled her grandfather saying, and it was true. She wove a quiver from strips of willow bark and tended her scarred foot and calf, gathering strength for what lay ahead. She missed Golden Eagle during the day, but haunting nightmares of the massacre rendered her nights sleepless. Then she would rise, sing, dance, and reaffirm her vow of revenge.

Thunder had no idea how far north she had walked until she awoke one morning to find snow on the ground. The forest lay hushed and beautiful. The delicate, lacy snowflakes reminded her of tiny spider webs, and the white snow clinging to the giant evergreens was breathtaking. In fact, it was so lovely, she failed to remember how dangerous it could be. She walked only a short distance before the wet snow soaked her moccasins, and her feet were freezing.

Removing the moccasins, she saw the bottoms had worn as thin as birch bark. Her missing toes reminded her to stop and take care of herself

Thunder sat on a rock ledge, letting the sun's warmth dry her moccasins. While waiting, she rubbed her feet, causing needle-like pains to shoot up her calves. She untangled her hair with a pointed twig, happy that it had grown longer. Her moccasins had dried by the time she finished grooming, and she set out. After a few hundred steps, her feet were freezing again. The ache was so distracting, she almost missed a plume of wispy smoke rising in the cold blue sky. Moving with caution, she darted from tree to tree until she reached a clearing and saw a small log cabin. Ignoring the pain in her feet, she crouched behind a tree and spotted a larger, dilapidated shed behind the cabin.

"Hurry, Ma," a young boy called from the shed in English.

"I'll be right there, Bobby," a woman responded from inside the cabin.

A door creaked open on the cabin's back side, and a sleepy-looking woman with a mass of tangled red hair emerged. She hurriedly carried a pail full of steaming water that sloshed over the rim with every step. Thunder smiled, wondering if any would be left by the time the woman reached her destination.

"Look, Ma, you can see the calf's head coming through." The young boy's voice cracked with excitement.

"Move over, honey. Let me see if I can help."

The old cow bawled pitifully.

Thunder sprinted to the front door of the cabin. Once inside, she swiftly scanned the room. Taking a folded blanket from the nearest cot, she spread it on the dirt floor. She placed a jar of salt, one of jam, and another packed with corn on it. She also snatched a loaf of bread, a small ham hanging from a wooden rafter, and many other miscellaneous items. She took only what she could carry with comfort. *Greed sometimes costs people their lives*, her grandfather had often said. She also took two rabbit skins hanging on a wooden peg near the fireplace. "New moccasins," she promised her feet.

When she finished packing, she tied the corners of the blanket together and slung it on her back. The cow bellowed again, so she peeked out a window. Through the shed's big open door, she saw the woman and the anxious boy, busily tending the birthing cow.

The woman frightened Thunder a little. She had never seen red hair and thought the woman might be a bad spirit. All appeared calm, however. She crept out the front door, crossed the yard in a flash, and sprinted into the mountains. Running at top speed, she did not slow until each breath became a stabbing pain. Her body accustomed to harsh treatment, she continued to run for many white man's miles before slowing to a walk. Gratitude for Blood Moon's instruction came to her. She had run efficiently without causing her limbs pain, the lack of air her only shortcoming. *The best I can do.* Unbidden thoughts surfaced of Blood Moon retraining her to run. *A good man, overtaken by more than he could bear.* The memory of that cold winter morning when he left the band brought a deep sadness to her heart.

The sun was sinking when Thunder found herself in a heavily wooded area. Judging this place safe enough, she halted, knowing she could easily slip deeper into the woods if necessary. She pulled a large chunk of bread from the blanket and used her fingers to slather it with jam. Taking a big bite into her mouth, she tried to swallow it too fast, and a fit of choking caused her to slow down. For the first time, she savored the jam's sweetness. In no time, her stomach was nearly full, and she rummaged through the rest of her bounty. Picking out a greasy yellow ball, she took a lick, then sank her teeth into it, enjoying the new taste. The yellow substance reminded her of rendered buffalo fat, but it was better. She wondered how the woman made it and decided to ask the next white people she met. Right before killing them, of course.

In the morning, the spirits in her head whispered that it was time for her to go. *Staying in one place can be dangerous*, they warned. She fashioned the rabbit skins into moccasin coverings and began walking again. She wondered if she should have killed the boy and his mother, but somehow, she felt their lives would not satisfy the spirits of her people. It was soldiers whom she needed to kill.

SEVEN

New Mexico Territory, April 1879

Facing the rising sun, Golden Eagle raised his coppery arms in unabashed prayer, thanking All-Father for the gift of another day. A tall young man of nineteen winters, he gazed at the heavens with eyes the color of a storm-clouded sky. With his head thrown back, his hair fell freely to his hips except for a single braid adorned with two gray eagle feathers. He was naked down to the waist but for the medallion of porcupine quills and blue and white trade beads hanging from his neck. He looked lithe and powerful in his deerskin leggings, breechcloth, and beaded knee moccasins. His strong, commanding voice rang out, slicing through the morning stillness like an arrow in flight.

In the soft light of predawn, a single star continued to shimmer, seeming to highlight the warrior's song:

Thank you, All-Father, for this new beginning.
Thank you for the mountains, the rivers,
The sky above and the air we breathe.
Thank you for the girl who talks like thunder.

As Golden Eagle sang, his hand drifted unconsciously to Thunder's medallion on his chest. He clasped the keepsake, and a mental picture of the young woman flashed before him. He sang the last words of his prayer-song: "Keep her safe, All-Father, until I find her."

The cold wind sighed through the buffalo grass and whipped strands of long, black hair across his eyes. Breathing deeply, he filled his lungs with the pine-scented air. Then he scanned the surrounding mountains for assurance that no soldiers followed him and his two friends.

Golden Eagle wondered how long it had taken the agent to realize they had stolen guns and escaped the reservation. Smiling, he remembered when, a half-moon earlier, Crossing Wolf and Two Feathers had distracted the sentries late one night. He had slipped into the horse barn, found three rifles with ammunition, and ridden out on a saddled horse, leading two others. He met his friends soon afterward, and they rode hard under the moonlight and throughout the next day. Now they were together and free.

During their captivity, they had learned a little English from interacting with the soldiers. They also worked with some plains tribesmen who taught them the sign language shared by many tribes. The Army paid them a negligible wage that most workers spent on liquor or gambling. The three braves mainly passed their time with the latter. They won more often than not and collected plenty of jewelry, beads, and turquoise to trade. By the time they completed the fort and returned to the reservation, Gray Fox and the others had already fled. The agency master had grown quite accommodating since then. According to reservation gossip, he had been reprimanded for starving the Indians and killing many as they escaped. The braves were stunned by the terrible news, certain many of their friends and relatives were among the dead.

While mourning, the three warriors bided their time. They milled around the huge reservation and met with people of other tribes. They traded their winnings for new clothes, war paints, and food, and kept some adornments for themselv—

Thwack! An arrow lodged into the earth near Golden Eagle's feet. He leaped back, much to the amusement of his comrades below.

"I have counted coup on you, brother," Two Feathers called, laughing. He was a year older than Golden Eagle, and two years younger than Crossing Wolf. He had proven himself a fearless warrior, but sometimes he acted like an overgrown boy.

"It is good, my friend," Golden Eagle said, "because you will probably never get close enough to count coup on an enemy."

"Two Feathers, as absurd as you are," Crossing Wolf remarked with a smile, "you should offer your services as a village contrary."

Golden Eagle pulled the arrow from the ground and said, "Enough kidding for now, my brothers. It is time to eat."

As Golden Eagle walked down the slope, he admired his comrades. Their long and heavy days of work at the fort had not

drained their resolve; instead, it had made them prouder to be Chiricahua warriors.

Crossing Wolf's keen eyes gleamed alertly in his broad-boned
face, and his wide nose hooked downward. His long black hair,
parted in the middle, hung freely from the deerskin headband, except
for one thin braid. From his scalp lock, two crow feathers hung sepa-
rately, each cut and painted to describe his honor of achievement. A
daub of black paint extended down each side of his face, from hair-
line to jaw. His deerskin shirt hung to mid-thigh. Draped over it was
a necklace decorated with badger's teeth, flat and wide; bobcat
incisors; and several sharp, narrow fox fangs. Some teeth were unde-
niably human. But the most outstanding adornment of all was the
long strand of wolf fangs, from which he drew his name and medicine power.

Although Crossing Wolf had only twenty-two winters, he walked
the path of the old warriors. He thrived upon discipline and order and
equated foolishness in a warrior with weakness. His temperament
often led him into clashes with the more modern-minded Two
Feathers.

Dressed in clothing of Mexican influence, Two Feathers wore a
shirt of yellow calico, and around his waist, he had tied a large red
sash. A beaded leather cord hung around his neck, and an ornate
copper band encircled his left wrist, protecting it from the twanging
of his bowstring. Buckskin leggings encased his legs nearly down
to his ankles, but opened in the back, partially baring the rear of his
thighs. His moccasins, trimmed in brightly colored porcupine
quills, had thick soles to protect his feet. A thin strip of leather
around his waist supported a sheath for a wicked-looking
butchering knife.

Golden Eagle smiled in gratitude for the companionship of his friends, well aware of the danger they would pose to their enemies.

After the braves returned to camp, they ate from their pemmican pouches, then mounted their horses and rode north toward the rendezvous point chosen by Gray Fox years earlier. At mid-morning, Crossing Wolf jumped to the ground and methodically inspected nearly indecipherable tracks. "Several weathered horseshoe prints, most likely from Bluecoats."

The three Apaches followed the tracks, which seemed to lead to Willow Creek. Golden Eagle's hopes of reuniting with his people steadily turned to dread at what he might find.

As they drew near the plateau, a sickly feeling of death and decay almost stopped his heart. The sight was horrific: bones and skulls strewn all over the burned-out remains of the village. Golden Eagle looked away, flinching, and saw the heartsick eyes of Crossing Wolf and Two Feathers. The three dismounted and surveyed the carnage in silence. Golden Eagle thought of his father who had nurtured him in his childhood and others who had molded him into a warrior. Now he could offer them nothing in return.

The three braves shuddered as they walked among the dead, looking at incomplete skeletons and torn clothing, partially covered by blowing dirt. Time and predators had rendered the dead impossible to recognize. Considering the chilly weather, Golden Eagle reasoned the massacre had happened between a half-moon and a moon earlier.

A piece of high-top moccasin caught his eye—his father's, he felt sure. He picked up the piece of buckskin that had held Grinning Bear's hidden skinning knife. After inspecting the now-empty sheath, he confirmed: *Father is dead, mutilated—his soul trapped.*

Tears of grief and rage burned his eyes as he saw his companions likewise standing over the remains of others. Had he been there for his father's death, he could have sent his soul to the underworld in peace. But this death, so wrong and untimely, brought a deep sorrow. *What can I do for him now? Only avenging his killers will set his soul free.*

In the early afternoon, Golden Eagle got up the courage to begin looking for Thunder. He inspected the entire village, praying he would not find anything of hers among the remains. Unable to know with certainty whether she lay among the fallen, he could only keep searching.

The braves wondered if any had survived the battle, but without knowing how many had escaped the reservation, counting the dead was of no use.

Crossing Wolf found a sandy indentation not far from the battle-field and thought it best to burn the bones there. They scoured the surrounding area for firewood and secured it to the horses' backs. Returning to the gravesite, they stacked the wood for burning. Most of the afternoon they spent in deep mourning, collecting the bones and remembering their lost loved ones.

Near where he had found his father's knife sheath, Golden Eagle discovered a thunderbird pendant, carved from sandstone. After picking it up, he studied it carefully, realizing someone had made it with great care and deep sentiment. He placed it among the pile of remains, where it could bring solace to the soul for whom it was intended.

At dusk, they started a fire and chanted prayers for the dead. With the fire at full blaze, they rode upwind from the village to camp for the night.

As they settled in, Golden Eagle's companions suggested that the soldiers might have captured Thunder, because of her uncommon beauty, rather than killing her. Golden Eagle refused to agree. He could not bear to think of the soldiers molesting her. He renewed his vow to press on and prayed to the spirits he would find Thunder free and unharmed.

When morning came, they returned to the gravesite to find most of the bones split and crumbled, leaving little to bury. They used their rifle butts to shovel the soft sand into a large mound and gave final respects to the dead.

After a time, they returned to concerning themselves with the living. Crossing Wolf suggested they fan out and search for tracks left by possible survivors. Downstream from the village, Golden Eagle noticed a small, well-concealed cave, its opening partially blocked by rocks. He drew closer and beheld a recently constructed tomb. Peering inside the big pile of stones, he saw Gray Fox's amulet lying on his bloodstained deerskin shirt. Sadness passed through Golden Eagle, but he was comforted by the realization that Thunder must be alive. *Who else would have made the effort to so carefully prepare Gray Fox's body for an appropriate burial?*

Wrapping himself in a shroud of memories, he recalled Thunder and Gray Fox riding into his village so long ago. She had clung to the neck of her horse as though she were sprouting from its back. He had felt her terror, although he could not see it, her pride too immense to betray her fear. He believed he had fallen in love with her at that very moment. He relished the power in her voice and her direct manner of speaking. No one could deny that something about her—her courage, her directness, her pride, her beauty—commanded the attention of others. None of those things mattered now. He only wanted to find her alive.

"Footprints," Crossing Wolf called from fifty paces away.

The others joined him. "I do not see footprints," Two Feathers said.

Crossing Wolf squatted and pointed at a shallow dent in the soil, and another one pace away, then yet another. "From big toes. We are lucky it has not rained since. But the tracks are old and faint; following the trail will be hard. The prints will be clearer in soft soil and wherever the ground is shielded from the wind. If I were her, alone, I would go deep into the mountains to be safe."

They headed northwest, seeing remnants of footprints on occasion. At mid-afternoon, Crossing Wolf spotted a disturbance in the sandy soil. A nearby ponderosa cast its long-plumed shadow over the ground, making it difficult to tell old signs from new. He slid down from his brown-and-white-patched horse and nudged it to move out of his way.

Golden Eagle and Two Feathers reined up, taking care not to disturb the sand. "What is it?" Golden Eagle asked.

"Overlapping moccasin prints. Someone must have rested here." Crossing Wolf bent down and picked up something. "Odd—a few strips of bark and bits of wood shavings."

"Wood shavings?" Golden Eagle asked, perplexed.

"Whoever it was tried to cover their trail but did not know how," Two Feathers surmised.

An image of Thunder flashed in Golden Eagle's mind. Remembering her prowess, he said, "Or could not take the time."

EIGHT

Colorado, April 1879

One morning in early spring, gloom cast itself across the land, and dark clouds pelted sleet on the Cheyenne village. Red Flower, aware of the ominous circumstance, kept her keen old eyes vigilant as she thought back to last summer.

The Cheyenne had escaped the reservation eight moons ago. As they traveled, the warriors had found a small herd of buffalo, killing enough to provide hides for lodges and meat for the cold season. They journeyed deep into the mountains and found an isolated spot near the Arkansas River that became their home for the winter. Throughout the moons of snow, Preying Wolf and the other elders discussed where to go in spring. Standing Tall had made strong arguments to search for his former Cheyenne band and its leader, White

Blade. "Certainly, if both bands unite," he had said, "all will bene-fit." With the snow now melted, the Cheyenne shared Standing Tall's restlessness to look for White Blade's band.

Red Flower's vigilant eyes caught movement. Searching the land through the icy rain, she saw figures in the distance moving fast toward camp. She pointed her gnarled finger to cavalry heading for them and called to warn the tribe.

Raven's Wing stood in the freezing rain, reassuring everyone. "Do not be alarmed by the soldiers' presence. We would all hate to return to the reservation, but we must remain calm. The Army has no reason to hurt us." When the troops grew closer, he slowly shuffled out to speak with them.

Bullets suddenly ripped into the ground near the old man. He stopped and raised his arms in surrender. Star and the others watched in horror as puffs of brown grass spiraled up around the shaman's feet.

Raven's Wing turned his head to Falling Star, looking her directly in the eyes. In his expression, she saw the love and power that came from many years of wisdom. She saw his knowledge of what was to come. She mourned. A bullet hit him in the chest, his knees buckled, and he fell dead.

Soldiers fired upon the warriors as they tried to establish a defense line. The women seized the children and ran into the wooded hillside. Accepting her mentor's message, Star slipped the medicine bundle on her back, clutched a small child under each arm, and followed the others.

Guns exploded everywhere, their blue smoke rising to the sky. Ragged heaps of humanity lay dark and dead on the frozen ground.

Those who remained on their feet turned this way and that before racing off in all directions. Still carrying the children, Star veered off at a bend in the stream. As she ran through a patch of briar bushes, a bullet slammed into her right upper leg. The impact hurled her backward, the children tumbling from her arms as she fell. Her head struck a half-buried rock, and she blacked out.

Sometime later, Star awoke, weak, dizzy, and disoriented, trying to comprehend why she was lying in a puddle. Raising a wet hand into view, she saw blood. As she struggled to sit up, a surge of horrendous pain shot through her leg. Peering down at her thigh, she found the source of the bleeding and immediately clamped both hands onto the wound. She looked around. Seeing many dead bodies brought back her memory of being shot. *What happened to the children I was carrying?* She did not see them or notice any sign of survivors. "All of my people dead?" she gasped. Grief seeped into her being, but she had to overcome it and save herself. With shaking fingers, she took a long, wide strip of leather from her pouch and knotted it tightly around the wound. She had lost a great deal of blood and knew she hovered near death. In too much pain to hold her thoughts together any longer, she fell back, unconscious.

When Star regained awareness, she realized the air had turned colder. Snow was falling, and it had drifted high enough to cover the sacred medicine bundle strapped across her back. She painfully sat up and looked around. *The battlefield will draw enemies, scavengers, and predators. I must leave.*

She focused on finding a walking stick and spied a rifle three paces away. Mustering all her strength, she dragged herself to the gun. She lay still until the pain subsided, then using the rifle as a crutch, she slowly rose to her feet. Again, she looked at the scores of dead littering the ground. *I can do nothing to help them. The soldiers killed everyone else, or someone would have returned to help me.* Planting the rifle barrel on the ground, she shifted her weight onto it, and hopped forward with her good foot a few moccasin lengths without jolting her injury. She moved her weight to her good foot, swung the rifle ahead, and planted the barrel on the ground again.

Star continued staggering along in this manner with little sense of time or distance. Blazing pain rendered her unable to do no more than keep moving away from the battlefield. Finally, the last vestiges of her strength vanished, and she collapsed.

Star roused to the sound of growling, and opened her eyes, seeing a wolf poised to strike. She spoke tenderly to the animal. He became silent, tucked in his tail, and disappeared into the woods. Despite great thirst, her fatigue forced her eyelids closed, and she drifted off once more.

When she awoke again, the dull sun clung to the earth's edge, waiting patiently to end the day. Recalling the battle, she wondered why the invaders had killed Raven's Wing and her people needlessly. She cried for the loss of her tribe as the light diminished and the harsh wind slowly abated. Finally, she forced herself to stop grieving and pushed herself up from the snowdrift and onto a dry embankment. Watching the night slowly settle around her, Star called softly to the vast, starlit sky, "Great Spirit, do not let me be meat for the wolves. Give me enough strength to get my bundle to where it belongs." Then she lay back and slept.

Partway through the night, she was stirred into semi-consciousness. Above her, she saw the outline of majestic antlers. Then she fell back to slumber, barely aware of the buck snuggling down beside her.

The next morning, Star came to with the certainty that something auspicious had occurred while she slept. *Was it a dream or a vision?* She tried for a long time to remember what had happened but could still only vaguely recall seeing elegant antlers. Her failure to remember more confounded her, but she had to turn her attention to survival. Cold and very thirsty, she needed to find water and shelter soon. With the aid of the rifle, she climbed to her feet and struggled forward. Pain forced her to stop repeatedly. When she could go no farther, she lay down in the snow on the leeward side of a fallen tree.

Star rested while the sun rose and set, hoping to regain some strength. Thirst overcame her. Although she knew eating snow would do more harm than good, she took a mouthful. Cold seared through her body, and she spat it out.

That night, she stirred into lightheaded awareness for only a heartbeat, feeling the heat from the buck's body. Then she drifted back to sleep, her memory of the deer gone beyond recovery.

She awoke at dawn, thinking only of finding a stream to cleanse her injury and slake her thirst. The wound, however, had gone bad. She tried to rise, but her upper thigh seemed to explode, and she stumbled and fell backward. Her head ached, and everything seemed fuzzy. She tried opening her eyes again, but the sun's glare on the brilliant snow blinded her. *Maybe it is not the sun. Maybe I am seeing Great Spirit's light.* Confused, she crawled to the base of a pine tree. Removing the binding from her thigh revealed a reddish-purple mound like a tiny volcano, ready to erupt. Exhausted, she wrapped her arms around her tucked knees. Emaciated and dehydrated, she alternated between burning fevers and freezing chills.

Still, she clung to a thin thread of life.

NINE

New Mexico Territory, April 1879

Toward evening, Golden Eagle's mare—lured by the scent of water—quickened her stride as she trotted up the winding path. Jagged chunks of broken granite jutted from beneath the thin layer of soil. Golden Eagle tightened the reins. One wrong step and the ledge could give way, sending horse and rider tumbling into the chasm. His knowing animal sidestepped again, leaped over a break in the granite, then trotted up the few remaining strides to a wide, flat area.

From below, Crossing Wolf called his name. He shouted back, "Up here! But be careful."

He slid from his mare's back to explore a small pool hidden in the overgrowth. Two Feathers and Crossing Wolf joined him and dismounted.

"It is late. Why not camp here tonight?" Two Feathers suggested, looking up at the clouded sky.

Crossing Wolf studied the surroundings. "Thunder, or whoever we are following, camped here."

"How do you know, brother?" Two Feathers asked. "There are no footprints in this stone."

Crossing Wolf laughed with an air of confidence. "See how these pine branches are arranged? Someone slept here among the leaves and used the branches to ward off the night breeze."

Golden Eagle turned from the pool to see for himself. *Yes*, he thought, *it looks like a sleeping place. Could Thunder have slept here?* Memories slithered from the shadows of Golden Eagle's mind of that cool evening he had spent with her on the trail. He remembered tasting her kisses and feeling the warmth they brought to him. His heart began a savage drumming. She was alive; he could feel it.

"There are many bad spirits in this place," Crossing Wolf cautioned. "We should leave before Father Sun does." He climbed back on his horse.

Golden Eagle looked at him. "How do you know there are bad spir—" A clap of thunder cut off his words, reverberating so loudly, the earth trembled.

Two Feathers mounted, instinctively tightening his fingers on the rawhide reins, and spoke sharply to his buckskin horse when she shied. Crossing Wolf drew his blanket over his head just as the sky opened and spilled water.

Golden Eagle quickly remounted. He wiped the rain from his eyes and squinted through the downpour, hoping to locate shelter, but he saw nothing in the fading light. The rain pelted him, stinging his body like a swarm of honeybees.

The drenched braves rode across the plateau for twenty bowshots until the horses became winded. Their hooves now sank into the soft, grass-covered soil.

Just before dark, they found an outcropping of stone large enough to offer protection from the wind and rain. The horses sank fetlock-deep in the muck as they trudged toward the shelter. Golden Eagle hated the sucking sounds of the horses pulling their hooves up.

They found nothing dry enough to make a fire, so they ate pemmican from their supply packs.

"The rain gods have verified your warning, brother," Two Feathers said with admiration. "It seems your power of knowing grows stronger."

"Perhaps, or it could be coincidence," Crossing Wolf said, "but I did feel many unhappy souls at that spring."

"Why are they gathered there?" Golden Eagle asked.

"Only a shaman could tell us that."

The next morning, they peered through wispy strings of fog to see the devastation the storm had wreaked. Large pine trees, spruce, and even ancient red cedars lay on the ground, their roots reaching toward the sky. The thunder gods had shaken the earth so violently that large chunks of sandstone had broken away from the cliffs and tumbled to the valley below.

Knowing the storm erased the tracks that may have been Thunder's, filled Golden Eagle's heart with despair. Regardless, he and his friends would return to the pool and look for any sign of the direction the traveler took. Without tracks, however, they had little chance of finding her.

TEN

Colorado, April 1879

After walking for many suns, Thunder found a dry creek bed with good flint for making weapons. She finished gathering the fragile stones, then collected sticks to make snares. After notching the larger sticks, she whittled the others into triggers and tied a rope to each of them. She found a game trail to place the first snare and pushed a notched stick into the ground. While pulling down a supple branch, she tied the free end of the trigger rope to it. After baiting the snare with corn from the cabin, she did the same with the other snares.

She returned to the creekbank, sat cross-legged and chipped the stones, grateful that Grinning Bear had taught her the skills of fashioning blades. By late afternoon, she had finished a razor-sharp cooking knife, and one of her snares had caught a squirrel. She thanked her prey for giving its life, then roasted and ate it. Her hunger satisfied, she started tanning the hide for an arrowhead pouch.

She worked tirelessly for the next three sleeps, making a hide scraper and arrowheads before attaching them to her set of mulberry-wood shafts. Not even a late-season snowstorm could hinder her progress.

The next morning, under a cloudy sky, she happened upon a game trail that meandered through the forest. The animal prints in the snow were so many, she could hardly distinguish one from another. Suddenly, the emerging sun revealed a series of dark brown spots. Bending down, she identified one.

"Blood!" she whispered in alarm. She calmed herself and considered the possibilities. *Likely from an old elk the wolves brought down.* She did not mind sharing with Brother Wolf—she only prayed he had left some.

Thunder looked ahead to see that the blood spots veered off the trail and entered the brushwood. The thought of fresh meat set a new pace for her feet. She hurried along a few steps until the hair on the back of her neck prickled in warning.

"There it is," she whispered. "It is a small deer!" She started forward but stopped abruptly. Something was wrong. Wolves would have eaten their prey where they caught it, not left a blood trail. *A hunter must have wounded this little doe, and it ran bleeding until it collapsed. Maybe the hunter hid upon my approach. If he is poised to shoot me, the other creatures will stay in hiding.*

Thunder dropped to the ground and lay as still as a fallen log. Keenly alert to any disturbance, she let her eyes wander through the dense tangle of undergrowth. For a time, nothing moved. Then, a curved-bill thrasher glided from the great, sweeping sky and landed on a high limb. After it began chirping, she spied a black-tailed jackrabbit digging a hole in the snow. Feeling safe again, she crept slowly through the brush and looked closely at the deer.

It is a girl wearing a deerskin dress!

Thunder rushed forward to examine the body, curled in the fetal position. *She will die without my help.* Her slight touch brought forth a pathetic moan. Leaning back on her heels, she looked more closely at the injured stranger. Wisps of long black hair veiled the gaunt face of a beautiful girl about a year younger than herself. *Her clothes have strange markings, and the ocher-dyed bundle strapped to her back must hold something sacred.*

She inspected the girl's body more carefully. A thin crust of dried blood drew her attention to the fleshy part of the right thigh. When she placed her fingers near the angry wound, she felt the searing heat. *Probably a bullet wound.* With no lesion of exit, the bullet must have remained inside.

"You are alive, strange one," Thunder whispered, "just barely."

Thunder removed the bundle from the girl's back, then slid the stolen blanket from her own shoulder and dumped its contents onto the ground. After wrapping the blanket snugly around the unconscious girl, she hurriedly gathered deadfall for a fire. *Enemies might see my fire's smoke, but I must take that risk.*

Scooping handfuls of earth with Grinning Bear's knife, Thunder dug a firepit, then lined it with small rocks and the deadfall. She struck one of her flints against the knife, and a spark shot into the pit. After carefully nursing the small flame into a scorching blaze, she put stones into the fire. Moving with sureness, she fashioned a tripod of forked sticks next to the firepit.

Thunder turned back to the girl and noticed something protruding from the blanket. Curious, she lifted the blanket to see a pouch tied to the stranger's side. Thunder untied the pouch and, to her surprise, found it filled with herbs. She pulled out the dried plants and sorted through the medicines. She realized with wonder and gratitude that the girl had collected the means for her own survival.

Thunder prepared a poultice of slippery elm, lady's bedstraw, and bear's foot. Together, they would reduce the girl's fever and combat infection. She also ground some of the plant of a thousand leaves and a portion of dry comfrey roots into powder. She put some of this into a poultice bag, kept more for treating the wound, and saved the rest for redressing later.

She placed Grinning Bear's knife in the fire for cleansing. Opening her rucksack, she brought out the buffalo paunch cook-skin that she had salvaged from her destroyed village. *Everything I need to prepare the herbs. Thank you, Ussen.*

Thunder emptied her canteen into the skin and hung it on the tripod. When the blaze died down, she used two forked sticks to lift and toss in a hot rock, causing the water to hiss and bubble. She added more hot stones until the water began to boil vigorously. She placed mugwort in the water and brewed it into a strong mixture to clean the wound before removing the bullet.

With the mugwort concoction, Thunder wiped clean the wound and the surrounding tiny mountain of tight skin. As a last effort to ensure her medicinal power, she chanted an old medicine song her grandfather had always sung:

> Great Medicine Wheel,
> Please speak to me today.

Great Medicine Wheel,
Use me to cure this girl in your way.
Great Medicine Wheel,
Grant me power to heal this day.

When Thunder slid the long, thin blade across the rotting flesh of the girl's thigh, a thick yellow pus spattered onto her face and arms. Grimacing, she bent forward, placed her lips on the wound, and sucked a mass of the vile liquid into her mouth. After spitting the fluid out with a disgusted grunt, she sucked more mouthfuls from the wound. Once she had drawn out all the pus she could, Thunder washed her mouth with the medicine broth, gargled, and spat. Taking a deep breath, she plunged the knife into the opening. She probed until she located the chunk of lead and popped it out. Next, she bathed the entire thigh and filled the wound with the various poultices she had prepared. Finally, she sealed the laceration with the glutinous ooze of comfrey and the thousand-leaved plant, then bound the area with dried comfrey leaves.

"Hia hia hia," she sang and danced the medicine song intermittently day and night. Her work appeared to be in vain, and on the third day, she had almost given up. She watched the feverish girl shivering and heard her teeth chattering the musical tune of death.

ELEVEN

New Mexico Territory, April 1879

Ol' Barney's burro sped up from his usual "don't-give-a-damn" pace when he caught the scent of mares corralled at the fort. He felt like a high-stepping stud now that the snow had melted and spring had sprung. He could feel nature's pull deep in his belly as he hurried forward to seek his male satisfaction.

Barney felt nearly the same. Neither he nor the burro had seen a female for months. An enormous grin spread across his wrinkled face as he passed through the heavy log gates of Fort Cauley. After dismounting, he pushed his way past the swinging doors of the fort's only saloon.

Settling into his favorite stool, he ordered a whiskey and downed it in an instant. A second whiskey soon followed the first. By his third drink, he recalled his manners and spoke to the bartender. "How's yer liver hangin', son?"

"Good as ever, you ol' coot. Ain't seen you around these parts for a while."

"Anything happenin' I orta know about?"

"Naw, winter's been pretty quiet. I bet them redskins is gonna start moving around now it's getting warmer."

"Reckon they will, all right. I already got a complaint to give Cap'n Baker." Barney tossed down the remains of his last shot, adjusted his bright red suspenders, and started for the door. "I'll be back soon as I sell my furs and take care a business," he called over his shoulder.

He walked across the muddy compound to the captain's home where he rapped on the door. Mrs. Baker answered, so he tipped his hat to her and inquired about Captain Baker. After exchanging greetings with the captain, Barney gave a report of all he had seen while out trapping and hunting. As he prepared to go, he said, "And by the way, Cap'n, Mary Browning asked me to tell ya somebody broke into her house an' stole a good bit of her food. Said her and Bobby were birthin' a cow in the shed and didn't see a thing. I took it 'pon myself to speak to her neighbor, John Linstrom. He claimed he saw an Injun girl running through them woods near his place. Said she was carrying some sort of bundle on her back."

"Did he say which tribe she belonged to?"

"Naw. He did say she probably weren't from around here, said her hair was short and her clothes real ragged and filthy."

"That is peculiar. The squaws around here all have long braids, and most of them are neat and clean. Listen, Barney, I'm short on men since I sent the cavalry under O'Riley to reinforce Colonel

Edwards' ranks. Nevertheless, tell Mary to get word to me if she has any more problems, and I'll get a squad of my new recruits up there."

"I'll keep my eyes open fer ya, sir."

"Thanks, and I'll be here if you need me."

Barney tipped his hat and departed. He whistled a happy tune as he headed back toward the saloon. He had money in his pocket and women on his mind.

TWELVE

Colorado, April 1879

For reasons unknown, the underworld seemed reluctant to relinquish the girl's spirit. After a fourth day of preparing and applying herbs, Thunder lay down, exhausted. With all expectations of saving the girl gone, she finally slept.

Thunder awoke to see the land veiled by a cloud of mist. Hungry, she made a fire, and warmed the turtle meat and gravy she had cooked the evening before, eating half. As the dawn sky lightened and the sun began to show its blood-red face, she knelt and prayed.

"Hou." The girl's voice cracked the silence like a whip. She looked across the firepit at Thunder.

"Aiieeeeeeeeeeee!" Thunder's voice boomed. "You have returned from nowhereland!"

The girl tilted her head to one side, a wondering expression on her face. Softly, she uttered a string of words Thunder did not recognize. She raised her body slightly and spoke again.

Thunder introduced herself. "I am Talks Like Thunder, Apache."

"I am Cheyenne, called Falling Star," the stranger answered in a language similar to Thunder's.

Thunder pieced together what she had heard. Bewildered, she asked, "How do you know a language so much like mine?"

Falling Star shifted again, transferring her weight to her elbow. Thunder saw pain in the girl's eyes. "While white men held my tribe in captivity, I made friends with a Navajo boy and learned his language."

Her curiosity satisfied, Thunder picked up the chunk of lead and held it out. "I took this from your leg. Do you remember being shot?"

Falling Star surveyed the vicinity with wary eyes before answering. "Yes, soldiers attacked us at our camp. I was shot and fell unconscious." A look of panic replaced her pain. "Oh, my bundle," she said in a rising tone. "Where is it?" She looked around wildly.

Thunder pointed to the bundle. "It is right next to you. I had to remove it to take the bullet from your leg."

Relieved, Star closed her eyes and murmured a phrase Thunder did not understand. *A prayer of thanks*, she guessed.

"Are you thirsty?" Thunder asked and gave her the canteen.

Star took a few swallows and offered it back.

"No," Thunder suggested. "Keep it near you to drink whenever you wish."

Star wrapped the string around the opening and set it down. "After the battle, I awoke to find all my people dead." Her voice trailed off, and deep furrows of pain lined her face. Her gaunt body quivered and crumpled back to the blanket. Her soft moaning tore at Thunder's heart. She knew too well the feeling of grief.

Thunder dished up a thin stone plate, piling it high with turtle meat and gravy. After sprinkling it with salt, she held it out.

Accepting the plate, Star took a few spoonfuls of the stew and began to speak again. "The bundle is all that is left of my clan."

"I am glad I did not open it," Thunder said. "Seeing the ocher-stained skin, I thought it might hold sacred objects."

Star gave her a grateful look. Overcome by fatigue, she put the plate down, closed her eyes, and drifted off to sleep. Thunder tucked the blanket around her, hoping the stew would restore her strength.

Before noon, Star opened her eyes again, and Thunder gave her more stew. Star took several bites, then began to speak, her voice stronger than before. As Thunder listened, Star explained how she had collected things that would keep the essence of her tribe. When she finished, Thunder indeed understood Star's commitment to bring her bundle to the remaining Cheyenne in the north. This reminded Thunder of her own vows, but she had to stay and help Star until the girl could travel alone.

"There will be time enough for revenge," she whispered to the wind.

The next morning, Star awoke to an empty camp. She panicked and called out to Thunder several times. The bundle, herbs, and cooking utensils—everything had vanished! She struggled to sit up and looked around wildly. A thin shaft of light seeped through the bare branches. No evidence of a camp remained. Confusion gripped her. *I must have been delirious and Talks Like Thunder a fantasy.*

A cold breeze stirred, causing Star to snuggle deeper into her blanket. "Wait!" she cried. "If I am hallucinating, where did I get this blanket?"

"From me," Thunder said, laughing as she stepped into the patchy sunlight.

Star sighed with relief. "I thought you had deserted me. When I saw the camp was gone too, I thought you were only a figment of my imagination."

"I went to find a safer place. It is too exposed here." Thunder pulled a pole drag from under a nearby bush.

Star marveled at her ingenuity. "Thank you, Thunder, for trying to help me, but I will not be able to get on the drag."

"I have a plan, if you want to try."

Since Thunder had already moved the rest of the camp, Star knew she had little choice. "I will do my best."

She cringed in pain as Thunder carefully rolled her onto her side and tucked one pole next to her. "I will roll you onto the drag. It will hurt, but it will be quick."

Star nodded, still wincing. As Thunder rapidly rolled her over the pole, the wound in her thigh exploded in piercing agony from skin to bone.

"Aiieeee!"

Thunder harnessed herself to the drag and began pulling. Though she avoided the roughest part of the mountainous terrain, the constant bumping along the rock-strewn path reopened Star's wound. Thunder stopped, removed the old poultice, and applied a fresh one.

Star felt the healing power of the plant of a thousand leaves through the poultice. As her pain lessened, she thanked the herb for bringing her back from the brink of death. She felt a reassurance from the plant of its friendship and loyalty.

As she watched Thunder work, she caught sight of scars on her arms and a tinge of sympathy overcame her. "How did you get those cuts?"

"They are mourning wounds. Bluecoats destroyed my village too." Thunder spoke flatly, leaving no room for questions.

After tending to Star, Thunder retied the harness around her waist and began pulling the drag once more. "I will have more respect for a pack horse in the future," she mused.

"And I, more compassion for the burdened."

A misty rain began to fall while Thunder veered from the path and began pulling the heavy pole drag up a short, steep bluff. Progress was slow and dangerous as they crossed an overhang jutting from the cliff's face, then angled down through a plum thicket to a narrow ledge. Finally, to Star's relief, Thunder halted and bent back a cedar branch that hid an opening in the stone.

"This is home," Thunder said, gasping. She leaned forward, pulled Star just inside the cave, and untied the harness from her waist.

Star looked around the cave as far as the light penetrated. The low-ceilinged chamber had enough space for them to store their possessions and rest comfortably. She caught an alarming smell, "The scent of a mountain cat!"

"I have inspected the entire cave," Thunder said. She reentered and kicked several old cat droppings outside. "That is what you smelled. The cave has been empty for days at least." She lit a small fire of cedar sticks to chase away the musky odor, then carefully rolled Star off the drag.

The next day, Star asked for wood so she could make bowls and cooking utensils. While carving, she realized just how well Thunder had chosen their hideout. Its southern exposure caught the afternoon sun's warmth, and a small mountain stream lay only paces away. The sweet water poured over a stone ledge and gathered in a bowl-like depression in the limestone. Star enjoyed sitting outside the cave and loved hearing the pattering of the waterfall. The fragrant aroma of the great ponderosa pines reassured her that the earth was fresh and clean. They had indeed located an ideal place, one with no people— only creepy crawlers, four-legged creatures, and winged ones.

Late one afternoon, as Star hand-fed a wren, Thunder whittled a heavy stick. "What are you doing?" Star asked.

"Sometimes when I check my snares, the animals are still alive. I need a club to instantly send them into the next life." Thunder paused. "It seems to bother you when I speak of trapping or hunting. Why are you so concerned with animals?"

Star did not answer right away. "In your village," she finally asked, "were you considered a warrior?"

"Yes, an apprentice warrior."

"In my village, I was a holy woman."

"Ah! That is why the Cheyenne consider your bundle sacred?"

"Yes, and I have a helper, a deer of spirit."

"My grandfather told me the spirits give everyone a spirit helper or animal totem. He said most people never discover theirs because only shamans and warriors go to seek them." She looked Star over and wondered whether this girl of fourteen winters could be a holy woman. "I suppose, if you were a real shaman, you would have supernatural powers."

"I am as real as the diamondback beside your foot." Star pointed to the snake as it started to rattle.

Thunder jumped up, holding her skinning knife.

"Put the knife down!" Star insisted. "Do you not know killing snakes brings ill-fortune? You must learn never to take a life unless you are saving one."

Star reached out and patted the rattler's head. The horny rings at the end of its tail quieted immediately. Speaking softly, Star asked the snake to seek another hunting ground. "Little brother, you frighten my friend and our horses."

Thunder watched, flabbergasted, as the snake uncoiled itself and slithered into a bush. *Supernatural powers can be used in any way the shaman wishes. I wonder how she does it.* Thunder spread her feet in the sand. "Is the magic in your hands or your voice?"

"Neither, my friend," Star said, laughing. "Sit with me, and I will tell you the story."

When Thunder had made herself comfortable, Star spoke of her unusual birth and explained the prophecy of a Cheyenne holy man called Sweet Medicine. She told Thunder of Raven's Wing, and how he believed the Great Spirit had sent her to save the Cheyenne way of life.

Considering her words, Thunder looked at Star's graceful, defined face, and her calm, empathetic eyes. *Yes, it is altogether possible. And that explains why plants and animals help her.* "Did I mention that the day I found you, I thought you were a deer?"

"Then you believe the deer provides me with foreknowledge and gives me a special connection with the animals?"

"Yes," Thunder said, smiling. "The deer is your totem."

The suns moved by rapidly, and with each passing, the respect and admiration Star and Thunder felt for each other deepened. Thunder snared rabbits and roasted them to perfection. Star made sewing needles from the rabbits' bones. She also tanned and stitched the skins together, to hang at the top of the cave's small entrance.

"Cheyenne believe you should never leave a lodge open," she explained to Thunder. "This symbolic barrier will keep away evil spirits."

During the next waxing and waning of the moon, Thunder proved an excellent provider. As Grandfather had taught her, she carefully honored every animal she killed for meat or hide.

Each girl mourned the loss of her family, but they comforted each other by telling stories and learning about the other's life. As they talked, they learned the other's language.

One day, Thunder shared with Star her puzzlement about the ways of the whites. "They kill us for our land," she said, angrily, "then persecute us while demanding we change our minds and hearts."

"There is something wrong with the whites," Star responded calmly. "They are children of the earth, like us, but they do not believe it. They think they must fight and beat the earth and everything in it until it serves them. In the end, they only fight and beat themselves."

"The whites are a scourge to us and the land," Thunder retorted. "If only Mother Earth would rid them from her realm!"

"Unlikely," Star said, gazing at Thunder with compassion. "They are still her children." Star looked strangely distant. "Perhaps they will change when they have no choice…"

June 1879

Thunder regularly came home to find Star doctoring creatures, from small cactus wrens to big desert rats, in the shade of a twisted palo verde tree that grew sparingly from a crevice in the rock. The animals approached fearlessly and ate crushed mesquite beans from her hands. She loved animals, and they seemed to feel the same about her.

One morning after they ate, Thunder said, "It has already been two moons since I found you, and you are healing quickly. Let us see if you can put weight on your leg. I will help you up."

Star shook her head. "To move my leg even a little is quite painful."

Thunder knelt down. "It will be just a test, and you can stop anytime."

Star sighed and looked questioningly at Thunder. "Yes, I should try." She raised her arm toward her friend.

Thunder placed one arm around Star's waist and draped her friend's outstretched arm behind her head.

"Be careful not to bump my leg," Star said as she leaned against Thunder, lifting her body with her good leg.

Thunder strained to readjust her balance to the added weight. "You are heavier than I thought."

Star gingerly put weight on her bad leg and barely lifted her other foot. She gritted her teeth, breathed heavily, and sagged into Thunder's body. "It is too soon," she gasped. "My leg cannot bear it."

"Let us get you back down," Thunder said encouragingly. "That was a good start. We will try again tomorrow."

"Thunder, thank you for saving my life, caring for me, and now helping me to walk again," Star said, teary-eyed. "I owe you my life."

Over the next several suns, Star began her first limping steps while placing much weight on Thunder. Within another moon, she could hobble about the camp alone. She kept herself busy by drying excess food or tanning hides. In the evenings, they made dresses, extra moccasins, and many other things they would need for their journeys. While sewing, they discussed everything from their different cultures to their innermost secrets. Thunder confided to Star her feelings for Golden Eagle. She told their entire story: their friendship, his rescuing her after the failed raid, and their intention to marry.

"What was your courtship like?" Star asked.

"I followed the custom of Apache maidens. I invited him to dance with me at the social dances and gave him a medallion I made."

"So, among your people," Star said in wonder, "it is the woman who pursues the man?"

Thunder smiled. "Yes."

"Do you initiate the marriage as well?"

"No, the man usually asks the woman's father first for her hand in marriage. Then, the man offers his gifts of horses. We had to do things a little differently: Golden Eagle proposed to me first. Still, we hoped to follow as much of our traditions as we could."

"That is much like what we do, except each family gives other gifts along with the horses," Star said. "A group of Sioux lived in our village for some years, and they had a delightful marriage custom. The day after the couple's families agreed to a marriage, they would have a marriage festival, feasting, and a ceremony."

"That sounds very different from our custom, and unnecessary. I just want to find Golden Eagle and be with him." Thunder smiled. "Our union depended only on my grandfather's permission and the gift of horses. With the change of circumstances, we will be considered married."

"So, you will look for Golden Eagle, even though it will be very dangerous."

"Certainly. And maybe he and his friends Crossing Wolf and Two Feathers will be looking for me too. We four are the only people left of our band."

"I hope to meet them someday."

The girls also spoke of their tribes' governing policies and religions. They soon discovered their religious beliefs had much in common, but their peoples held very different ways of choosing leaders.

The Apaches had no governmental organization. They relied on a self-appointed *nantan* who always dedicated his life to his followers. Often, a *nantan* would not eat until every widow and orphan in the village had food. When returning from a raid, he usually gave his share of bounty to the poorest families, keeping little or nothing for himself. A *nantan* had a patient ear, listened to every problem, and was often called upon for a just solution.

Apache war leaders appointed themselves as well. Any warrior could plan a raid of his own. He had only to invite other warriors to join him. If they accepted his invitation, he led them for that raid only. Chiricahua hunting and trading expeditions were handled in much the same way.

The Cheyenne, Star claimed, lived very differently. They had a very complex political hierarchy, including war chiefs, peace chiefs, principal chiefs, and sub-chiefs. Her people elected all their chiefs. They did not appoint themselves.

Though intrigued by the differences in their cultures, each respected the ways of the other. While they talked, they kept their hands busy. They wove baskets of buffalo grass and willow branches, each fashioning her own unique designs.

One evening, Star put down her basket and said, "Thunder, my people know of a country far to the north where we can live freely as we always have. I wish to go there after I have given my bundle to the Cheyenne. Once you find Golden Eagle, would you like to join me in my quest?"

Thunder continued weaving. "With or without Golden Eagle, I must take revenge on the Bluecoats. It will not be long until I begin taking scalps, and several moons before I leave this land to go with you."

"I am certain you will not find your revenge as satisfying as you believe. But I have no power to stop you."

As Star's leg mended, she and Thunder began spending afternoons walking in the forest. Since the Season of Large Leaves had arrived, they gathered a variety of roots and medicinal plants. On rainy days, Thunder helped Star dry meat, berries, and herbs. They created many colors of dye, which they used to decorate their clothing. Light red they made from sumac berries, and sunny yellow from boiled goldenrod blooms. Before long, they had also perfected various shades of blues and browns.

Thunder returned from hunting one afternoon to discover Star painting white images of animals deep within the cave walls. Thunder was astonished. She had never seen a power or spirit symbol affixed to stone. But the old ones in her village had spoken of visionaries who could do this. Near the entrance, Star's largest drawing of a white buffalo, aroused Thunder's particular interest. On very rare occasions, hunters had seen a white buffalo in a herd. Regarded as sacred, white buffalo signified the regeneration of humanity. When Thunder reached out and touched the image, her body went rigid, and everything faded.

In dim twilight, Star ran down a steep incline, darting from side to side, with something bulky strapped to her back. Another Indian girl followed her as they both tried to evade two mounted soldiers. The horsemen aimed their rifles at the girls, and fire erupted from the ends of the barrels...

Thunder frantically jerked her hand back. The vision faded, and a burning sensation spread from her palm to her fingertips. "Star!" she cried, her voice no louder than a croaking frog.

"Thunder?" Star lurched awkwardly to her feet. "What is the matter?"

"I am not sure. When I touched the white buffalo image, I saw you and another Indian girl running near soldiers."

Star's expression grew serious. "It sounds as though you had a vision."

"I thought only seers had such medicine powers."

"No, anyone can see."

"See what?"

"You know—see something that has happened in the past or will happen in the future."

Thunder had only a vague notion of what her friend meant. She had known Apache warriors who went in search of visions. A boy had to complete this rite, and others, before his people considered him a man. He would go into the mountains alone, with no food or water. The elders required him to remain there for four sleeps, or until he found his own animal totem or medicine from which to obtain power. Thunder had never heard of power coming to seek an individual as it had come to her. Star's power in the fresh paint had given her the vision. Thunder had always had a vivid imagination, but this vision frightened her. Even more alarmingly, it seemed to foretell danger for her friend.

July 1879

The end of the Moon of Red Cherries found Star healed completely, aside from a slight limp.

One evening, just before dark, Thunder returned with an armload of willow twigs and greeted Star. She paused when Star did not speak or look up from her cooking.

"Is something wrong, sister?" she asked.

Star slid a crusty brown quail off the roasting stick onto a yellowish clay plate, which she handed to Thunder. "My friend, my heart aches to think of leaving you and our wonderful home. However, you must go south to avenge your people and find your love, and my duty is to bring my bundle to my people."

Thunder had always known this time would come, but she had not anticipated such pain in their parting. She had never known any other girl like Star. A desolate feeling arose at the thought of life without her friend.

Star spoke again. "It is not something I want to do—it is something I *must* do."

Thunder looked up and grew unnerved by the pain in her friend's eyes. "I understand. I have an obligation too."

"It is settled. We will pack everything tomorrow, and we should be ready to leave at dawn the next morning."

Thunder nodded her head and lowered her face to keep Star from seeing the tears welling in her eyes.

The next afternoon, over an outdoor fire, Star busily prepared all of Thunder's favorite foods for their last meal together. While stirring the bubbling stew, she glanced uneasily at the sinking sun. "It is getting late," she muttered. "Thunder should be back from checking snares by now."

The prairie chicken, cooking with wild turnips, onions, and mushrooms, gave off a rich, tantalizing scent. Star tilted her head back and sniffed the pungent aroma, almost enjoying the hunger pangs it evoked. While she waited, a vague uneasiness disturbed her. Tension surged through her body. Something was very wrong.

"Thunder," she called, "where are you?"

Hastily inspecting the camp, she found everything neatly packed and ready for their departure. She saw nothing to alarm her, yet her unease remained.

Suddenly, a gigantic deer appeared three paces before her. The buck stood calmly, his huge liquid brown eyes staring directly into hers. Star, taken aback, froze and awaited counsel. The animal spoke to her without sound, sending a clear command into her mind. *Go in haste! Kill the attacker before he kills your friend!*

A scream shattered the silence. A cold hand seemed to tighten around Star's heart, raising the hair on her neck and arms, a prickly sensation like Grandfather Spider crawling up her back.

Instinctively, she grabbed her knife and leaped into a sprint. Another scream rent through the air, a frantic cry of agony that she recognized as Thunder's voice.

"Please, Maheo, do not let her die," Star prayed as she tore through the thick underbrush. Desperation drove her toward the dreadful screams. *If I had the power of Sweet Medicine, I would already be at Thunder's side, helping her fight the enemy.* Choking back panic, she darted forward, dodging trees and ducking limbs.

A third scream, this time very close. Star hurried toward it.

"Hold still, you little bitch!" a man's voice shouted just ahead.

Star stopped, crouched low, and pulled aside branches of a thick-leaved bush. Thunder lay on the ground, pinned beneath a huge white man, her dress ripped open from hem to waist. Flailing desperately against the man, Thunder gripped his wrist with both hands, keeping his knife from plunging into her throat. Star dashed forward and, without a thought, buried her knife in the back of the man's neck. Blood gushed from him, spurting onto Star's dress and raining down on Thunder's face. The man began to raise his head, then collapsed on top of Thunder.

Twisting her body and pounding powerfully at the big, heavy corpse, Thunder shoved it partially off her, freeing her flailing arms.

Star knelt and tried in vain to grab her wrists to calm her down. Thunder continued to thrash her clenched fists, pelting Star with hard blows. *Thunder might seriously hurt either of us if I do not stop her now.*

Star grasped her friend's arm, but Thunder wrenched it away, her unseeing black eyes defiant. Star grabbed both her wrists and held them down with all her strength as garbled words poured from Thunder's mouth.

"Thunder! It is over!" Star shouted. Her forceful tone and her hands clamped onto Thunder's wrists brought the girl back to awareness, and she stopped struggling. The man's unmoving body still covered her stomach and legs.

Star stood and shoved her foot into the man's hip, rolling him over. The corpse lay on its back, spread-eagled on the dirt. *What a despicable man! Such a lowly soul, unaware of how he scourged Thunder and himself. What can I possibly tell her?* Staring at the corpse, she took a deep breath. "Thunder, nothing you could ever do would bring about such evil. I cannot provide you a reason for what happened." Turning her eyes to Thunder, she saw her friend's suffering and knew she had not heard a word.

Freed of the man's weight, Thunder rolled to her side and spat repeatedly, as if trying to remove the coppery taste of the man's blood from her mouth. Tears from her shame-filled eyes left muddy tracks down her raw, dirt-caked face. Her eyes glazed over as she fainted.

∿

Thunder awoke to the sound of Star's voice calling her name. Hands cradled her tender face, bringing a sting of pain. Opening her eyes, Thunder saw Star gazing at her in sympathy and turned away, ashamed.

Slowly getting to her feet, Thunder felt pain radiate from deep inside her abdomen. As she took small, hesitant steps, blood ran down the insides of her thighs. Thunder hunched her head low into her shoulders like a turtle. Feeling defiled, she yearned to wash off the man's filth that instant. Her torn, bloodstained dress unfurled as she staggered about.

"He is dead," Star reminded her.

"Good," Thunder croaked. The man's choking grip had bruised and swollen her throat. She swallowed convulsively, trying to remove the constriction in her gullet. Thunder stared at the bloody foam bubbling from the man's mouth, clotting in the dirty brown hair covering his face. His blue eyes, behind half-opened slits, still mirrored his shock. She drew back her leg and kicked him, then jumped back from fear he might reach out and grab her. Seeing her knife on the ground, Thunder picked it up. She stooped over the man, hacked off his manhood, and crammed it into his gaping mouth.

"I hope it stays in your throat forever!"

Thunder watched Star retrieve her knife from the man's neck and cut his tendons to further incapacitate him in the next life. Then, she severed his filthy scalp and held the nasty thing at arm's length. "Do they never bathe?"

"Does not smell like it," Thunder replied, nauseated by the odor. She waved for Star to take the scalp away.

Star flung the gory mess downhill into the brush. "How did he find you?"

"I do not know." Thunder rubbed the bump on the side of her head. "When I struck a weasel caught in my snare, he knocked me unconscious from behind. When I came to, his knife was at my throat…" She could not finish the sentence. A searing blister of shame stole her voice. *How can I ever face Golden Eagle again?*

"I am so glad you held him off until I arrived." Star gently placed her arm around Thunder's shoulder and felt the horror of what just happened to her friend. *It must be unbearable for her. First, the invaders killed her people. Now they have violated her body and taken her dignity.* "Let us go home, Thunder."

In the distance, a horse whinnied. Star looked around—the sound had come from a grove of trees below. "We must find that horse," she whispered urgently.

"I will stay here," Thunder mumbled.

"I will not leave you by yourself." Star pointed downhill to a grove. "There may be more white men. Come with me."

Star took several steps before noticing she was alone. She looked back, troubled to see Thunder shuffling along, withdrawn and disconnected, her torn dress flapping in the breeze.

Star slowed her pace as they crept toward the grove, their moccasins pressed silently against the soft ground. After tiptoeing down a slope into a copse of sycamore, they sneaked into its obscure shadows.

A beam of sunlight slanting through the trees illuminated a small, well-concealed camp. A gelding and a little bay mare stood, watching the girls weave in and out of dark patches of shade. As they drew near, the gelding snorted and lifted his head, pulling harshly at the leather strap binding him to a tree. Beside him, the mare shifted her weight and remained silent. Star strained her eyes, anxiously waiting for someone to appear. Several moments passed, with no sign of movement in the camp. Star motioned for Thunder to follow her.

As they stepped into the small clearing, a hawk circling overhead gave a bloodcurdling shriek. Star stopped and carefully observed her surroundings.

A tent-like shelter made of buffalo hides was held upright by four poles. From the untrampled grass around it, Star surmised someone had pitched the camp a day earlier. A burnt-out fire occupied the center, and a pot hung from a spit above it. A pile of furs lay in a tumbled heap in one corner, and the rest overflowed with assorted supplies. A saddle, a willow pack frame, and a holstered rifle lay in front of the furs.

Thunder wrinkled her nose and whispered, "What is that awful odor?"

"Something is in here." Star removed the heavy iron pot from the spit and tipped it over, dumping a blackened mass onto the ground. Her stomach turned at the sight of the heap of charred beans. Choking back the disgusting taste of gall in her throat, she said with a feeling of certainty, "The man was a trapper, and he rode alone."

Thunder rubbed the hairless spot on the gelding's back. "Are you sure?"

"There is only one saddle, so the gelding carries the pack frame. We must leave this land. I think we should load these provisions on the gelding."

"Can we just go home?"

Star looked at her friend, aware of her shame, desolation, and yearning for peace. "I assure you, Thunder, we will go back home soon. But dead whites bring more whites. We should search the camp now before they can get here. It will not take much time. We do not know what lies ahead. I see your pain, but we need to take these provisions and ride away at sunrise. This food will allow us to stay on the move and keep us safe."

Thunder looked around. "Did your people not get the pox and die after Broken Lance took the whites' provisions?"

Star frowned at the thought of the loss of her people, but quickly composed herself and smiled. "I admire you for remembering that at a time like this. That did happen, but now the plant of a thousand leaves will warn me if there is danger. I trust his spirit."

Thunder apathetically pilfered the supplies, while Star did most of the work. She saw no use for the coffee or bottles of liquor they found. However, she took the honey, dried meat, small sacks of flour, and burlap bags. In moments, they stuffed the supplies into the bags and tied them to the pack frame on the gelding. Star removed two buffalo skins from the shelter and covered the packs, leaving barely enough room for Thunder. The mare appeared calm, but Star saw the gelding roll his eyes, a definite sign of trouble.

Thunder languidly approached the gelding, then took a firm grip on the rope halter and another on the horse's long chestnut mane. After swinging herself up, she squeezed in among the packs. The gelding shied, unaccustomed to orders coming from a pair of knees gouging him in the ribs. He dropped his head and started bucking, his twisting back flinging her from side to side.

The horse battered Thunder against the packs until she lost her grip. She fell, landing amid his pounding feet. Somehow, she remained unscathed as the gelding burst into a run. The packs ripped to pieces, their contents scattering everywhere.

"You no good horse of a jackass!" Thunder shouted. "I should have known you would be just as stupid as your master!"

"Oh, no!" Star said as she scurried over. "The fall must have sorely hurt you after what you have suffered." She reached out. "Are you all right?

Thunder took Star's hand and got to her feet. "The fall just bruised my ribs and burned my rear."

As they repacked, Thunder said, "We can catch the idiot horse after he runs himself out." She pointed to a bluff. "The mountain on the other side of these trees, only a short bowshot away, has a rugged rock base. That will be a good place to dump the trapper's stinking carcass."

They dragged the body to the bottom of the granite mountain and looked for an opening.

"Sometimes the predator becomes prey," Star said as they shoved the man into the widest fissure they could find.

Thunder rolled back her head and howled long and loudly. "Come, brother wolves, your dinner is waiting!" Her weird laughter echoed eerily in the dusky twilight.

THIRTEEN

Colorado, July 1879

Leading Thunder back to the trapper's camp, Star saw the skittish gelding had returned. It stood next to the mare, nickering softly.

"Let me try him this time," Star said. She approached and instantly won the horse's confidence with her soft, crooning voice. She mounted the gelding and rode him over to where Thunder waited. "Hand up those packs and skins," she said, grinning sheepishly.

After a short ride to their campsite, the girls dismounted. They freed the horses of supplies and riding gear, letting them graze.

"I am going to the stream to bathe," Thunder told Star, who followed. Thunder stepped into the water, peeled off her torn dress, and halfheartedly rubbed at the bloodstains, to little effect. Star removed her dress and saw how bloodstained it was. Both dresses would always remind them of this day. Thunder stared blankly into the water. Star realized the shock of the attack had now sunk in, leaving her friend numb and injured. *I will need to stay with Thunder to help her heal. It will take a long time; I should start now.*

They wiped the excess water from their bodies with the wet dresses and returned to camp. Star went into the cave and emerged with two new dresses and pairs of moccasins. They dropped their wet clothes and donned the dry dresses.

Star slipped on a pair of moccasins, then picked up the other pair and held them out to Thunder. "Here, put these on too."

Thunder tossed the moccasins in front of her and slid them around with her toes. "I will put them on later. I need to rest for a while."

The sight of her friend, so helpless and vulnerable, tore at Star's heart. The desolate expression on Thunder's face marred the clean, straight lines of her nose and cheeks. Her jet-black eyes, lifelessly gazing to the horizon, mirrored the suffering in her soul.

Star hugged Thunder and whispered, "I will not leave to find the Cheyenne. Not yet. I will stay here with you. Together, we will be safe."

Star gave Thunder an extra squeeze and felt her friend's body tremble as the girl broke down and wept. For a long time, they stood in the embrace, Thunder crying uncontrollably, and Star weeping with her.

As Thunder began to calm down, Star helped her to sit, then went to the woodpile. She took all the logs, stacked them high, and started a fire at the base.

Evening had come by the time the wood burned at a full blaze. Star retrieved her wet dress and moccasins, then assisted Thunder to her feet. "Come," she said. "Pick up your old clothes and follow me."

After they reached the fire, Star looked into the flames and recited healing chants. She threw in her discarded clothing. "May the Great Devourer take the wickedness of this day and transform it for the good."

She gestured to Thunder, who flung her moccasins and soiled dress onto an upright log in the fire. "For the good?" Her pent-up anger flared. "I hate the man who defiled me! Star, why did you not just wound him so I could have killed him myself?"

Star turned her somber eyes to the fire and spoke calmly. "Watch the fire purify the symbol of today's evil deed."

The dress hung from the log, curling and sizzling, giving off an eye-watering stench. Then, it fell into the red-hot coals. When no trace of the dress remained, Star said, "It has left us, just as the life of the man."

The next morning, Star took some food from their packs and prepared stew. While dishing up the meal, she saw Thunder braiding her hair, as if trying to reach back to her childhood innocence. She held a bowl out to her friend, who pushed it away.

"I am not hungry."

Star nodded. "I understand, but will you eat with me later today?"

"Maybe a mouthful." Thunder continued working with her hair.

"You told me you hated your braids when you were at the school."

"Today I do not feel like a warrior. I am braiding my hair for now, and I might cut it off."

"Your braids look fine. Why would you cut your hair off?"

Thunder's eyes flashed at Star. "I do not need your permission!"

Star shrugged. "Of course, you do not," she said flatly. "It is just beautiful hair, that is all." She began cleaning the cooking utensils. "Why not start packing? We will head south to find Golden Eagle."

Thunder looked at the ground and mumbled, "I do not want to see him."

Gently, Star thought. *Naturally, she does not.* "Maybe we will not find him, but we should try."

"I would prefer not finding him. I am no longer an untouched maiden. Golden Eagle could refuse me, and I would not blame him."

"Let us ride south," Star said with a lightness she did not feel, "and let the spirits decide."

Thunder finished braiding her hair and slowly nodded.

After they loaded the horses, Thunder said, "I will take the gelding." She jumped onto his back, turned him southeast, and cantered away.

Star smiled, thinking her friend would recover in time. She mounted the little mare and sped to catch Thunder.

While they rode, Thunder described how vulnerable she felt after the trapper's attack and her relief that people would not gossip about her. Star listened and continued to encourage her friend to talk about anything she wished. Star knew Thunder needed more than a friend. She needed someone who understood her as intimately as she knew her own self. The more Star learned of Thunder's every thought, every fear, the more she could help her.

At mid-afternoon, they stopped to rest on a wooded knoll. Star lit a fire, then unpacked their dried food. Thunder took the rifle from its scabbard, then rummaged in one of the trapper's packs, pulling out a Colt .45.

"Look at this. The reservation guards carry guns like this. Have you ever seen one?"

"Some of our warriors had pistols," Star answered as she hung pots of food over the fire.

"Do you know how to shoot it?"

"No, but I can figure it out."

Thunder held up the rifle. "Which do you prefer?"

"The one you do not choose. Keep it until I need it. Since your path is vengeance, you will need the rifle, will you not?"

"Yes, the bullets fly much farther." Thunder cocked the rifle. "It is not loaded." She picked up the pistol. "Nothing in this one either." She got up and stepped to the gelding. "Star, did you find ammunition at the trapper's camp?"

"No. Why not look near where the guns were?"

Thunder searched through the packs. "I do not see any."

"I am sure I would have remembered seeing shells. Maybe the trapper hid them, worried you would find his camp and use his guns against him."

Thunder returned the guns to the packs. "We may find bullets for them later."

Thunder's fascination with the trapper's weapons must have given her an appetite. To Star's surprise, she ate half of her meal.

Riding out from their afternoon camp, they crossed a nearby meadow.

"Thunder," Star ventured, "I have to confess—I feel guilty. I should have gone with you to check your snares as soon as I could walk. That might have prevented the attack."

"Please do not feel guilty. I am sorry I yelled at you for killing the trapper last night." She glanced at Star, then quickly looked away.

"No, Thunder. It was good for you to speak your mind."

"With your aversion to taking life," Thunder said in a serious tone, "how do you feel about killing the trapper?"

Star shifted in her saddle. After collecting herself, she told Thunder how the deer had appeared and told her to kill the man. "I just obeyed my deer totem. Besides, the trapper had no care for others, so he brought his death upon himself. I was merely the spirit's instrument to deal justice."

"Whatever the reason, I am glad you saved my life."

Star shrugged and answered simply, "You saved mine." Inwardly, however, she was happy Thunder still valued her life.

New Mexico Territory, July 1879

They traveled along a river for several suns, living off the trapper's rations. One evening, unable to tolerate another meal of the disgusting food, Thunder went in search of fresh meat. She returned, disappointed and angry, the ends of a broken string dangling from her bow. She would have to find yucca plants, pound and wash the fibers, and dry them before she could restring her bow.

Late the following afternoon, while riding along a game trail, Thunder told Star, "I need to stop early tonight to fix my bow."

Star abruptly halted without responding and threw out her hand.

Thunder stopped her horse and snapped her head around. "What is wrong?" she asked in a low voice.

"Someone is over there." Star pointed to the river's bend two bowshots away.

Perplexed, Thunder glanced at the river. *How could Star have heard anyone from so far-off?* Leaning forward among the packs, she whispered, "How do you know?"

Instead of answering, Star yanked upward on the reins. Turning the mare abruptly, she rode to the cover of oak trees, and Thunder followed closely behind. When they dismounted inside the grove, Thunder could no longer restrain her curiosity. "What happened out there? Why do you think someone is at the river?"

"My deer totem told me."

They led the horses to a deep ravine and securely tied them to a tree.

The ability of Star's totem to help her in ways beyond normal human powers amazed Thunder. *Maybe I could someday discover my own totem and receive such help from the spirit world.*

The girls crept to the river, then moved noiselessly across the sandy soil to the river's bend. From behind a cover of thick foliage, they heard voices. Carefully, they parted the grass and saw five soldiers across the river, making camp for the night. Thunder gestured for Star to remain hidden, then slipped upriver to scout the area.

Father Sun had gone to rest by the time Thunder returned. Her dark eyes flashed with excitement as she signaled for Star to follow.

They walked deeper into the shelter of trees before Thunder whispered, "It is Stormy! The soldiers have my Stormy!"

Thunder did not need to explain what she meant. She had told stories about the wondrous horse since she had met Star. "I must have him back!" she declared, her voice still low. "Will you help me?"

"We have no weapons, and the soldiers outnumber us," Star whispered skeptically. "What is your plan?"

"We kill the soldiers with our knives, then take Stormy and the other horses. This may be my only chance to get him back."

Far to the north, a bolt of lightning arced between two clouds. Star pointed to it and said, "That is a bad omen. Though it is your namesake, thunder will ruin any sneak attack. Please reconsider attacking the soldiers."

"Tonight, it is time for vengeance," Thunder declared, ending the discussion.

Star shrugged her shoulders and gave Thunder a look of exasperation.

As the girls sat chewing dried meat from their packs, the first pale rays of moonlight shone through the trees. Thunder, still ecstatic, described the countryside. "Across the river, one bowshot upstream from camp, the tree-covered land opens to a meadow. The soldiers are keeping the horses there in a rope corral." She drew a map in the dirt to outline her plan.

"We will leave our horses where they are," she instructed. "I will cross the river here," she pointed to her map, "and you cross upstream, near the corral. It will be easy. No rain for days, so the current is slow. I will signal with an owl hoot when to cross. I will take out the night guard while you circle around. When I am ready, I will send the signal again. We will attack at the same time and kill them all. Then, you take the horses across the river and meet me at the ravine."

Star hesitated. "Isn't this plan a little rash and unnecessary? You should be satisfied with taking the horses."

"After what the trapper and the soldiers did to me and my people?" Thunder hissed. "I must take revenge!"

"Trying to take these men's lives needlessly may bring us to our deaths," Star insisted.

Thunder clamped her jaw shut and released a labored breath. "They killed all my people without pity and deserve to die. If you refuse to help me, I will do it myself."

"It is against my nature to kill unsuspecting men. But you will surely die trying to kill five soldiers with only a knife. Since you are adamant, I will help you."

Thunder looked at her with mouth agape. *I forgot about her aversion to killing.* Recollecting herself, an idea came to her. "After I kill the sentry and have his rifle, I will signal with a double owl hoot. Then, you stay away, and I will shoot them all. If only a single hoot, we will stay with our first plan. Wet clothes will hamper our movements, so we will cross naked."

Star paused for a moment. "Sorry, Thunder, I must keep my clothes with me."

"The river is no more than chest high. You can walk across."

"Are you suggesting I carry my clothes over my head?"

"Yes. I will hide mine at the ravine now. Wait here."

"So, you will attack them naked?"

"Of course," Thunder called over her shoulder, barely audible, as she ran off.

When the gray twilight deepened into moonlight, Thunder returned from concealing her clothes. The lightning was now close enough for them to hear thunder faintly rumbling.

"A thunderstorm will make our raid much more dangerous," Star whispered. "Let us settle on just taking the horses."

"After you agreed to help, you cannot back out now!" Thunder crept to the riverbank, glad the conversation was over. *Why can Star not stop harping about calling off the raid? At night, these soldiers are like blind moles.* She hid among the tall cattails and looked back. As planned, Star took off up the river, toward the corral. Turning, Thunder saw the soldiers by the light of their fire, only fifty moccasin lengths away. The soldiers puttered around, getting situated for the night.

The fire burned down, leaving barely enough light to see four of the men crawling into their bedrolls. Soon, the quiet night gave rise to snores. A young sentry paced at first, but eventually sat back against the base of a cottonwood tree, his rifle balanced on his lap. The huge tree grew half in, half out of the turbid water. Thunder watched the boy's head drop to his chest. In moments he lay still, aside from the deep, slow rhythm of his breathing.

She gave forth an owl hoot, telling Star it was time to cross.

Knife in hand, she waded silently, other than her faint swishing from the rippling water. A cool breeze hit her, but she continued to quietly move forward. Coyotes moaned a sorrowful tune, rising and falling in the distant hills. Crickets chirped, and owls hooted. The night sounds reassured her that no one noticed their approach. She ducked underwater and swam toward the sleeping guard.

When Thunder stood, slick mud sucked at her feet. Taking great care to make no sound, she bent down and scooped a handful of the muck. This she smeared over her entire body, to darken her and kill the human scent. The sentry's rifle barrel protruded horizontally from the other side of the tree. *Good. It is still on his lap.* She climbed up the bank on hands and knees and crawled around the cottonwood to the sentry.

She sat on hunched knees, an arm's length from the guard's side, studying his blank face in the moonlight. He looked too young and innocent to be wearing a murderer's uniform. As Thunder turned the skinning knife over in her hands, Star's words about needless killing echoed in her mind. She cringed, remorse filling her, and she wondered if she could silence the young soldier without killing him. She dropped the knife behind her, then encircled his neck with her arms, clamped one hand over his mouth, and pinched his nostrils shut with the other. The boy awoke with a start. He flung up his arms; his gun tumbled into the air, toward the river. Thunder quickly slid her body against his back, out of reach, still holding his nose and mouth. She heard the gun hit the bank and roll downhill until it plopped into the water. *Damnation! I really needed that rifle!* The sentry grabbed her wrists and pulled against them, but she used all her strength to hold firm. The boy jerked and clawed at the air for a few moments, then crumpled and grew still.

Thunder lowered him to the ground, thinking she had killed him. Then, she saw his chest expand and contract. Quick as a wink, she searched for his pistol but found only a belt on his waist. She removed it and bound his wrists and feet together. Seeing a handkerchief protruding from his pocket, she stuffed it into his mouth.

She gave forth a single owl hoot, telling Star they would abide by the original plan.

Thunder grabbed the knife and crawled to the sleeping men. She heard a deep rumbling from the clouds, loud enough to wake the soldiers. *Oh, no! Star was right. I must signal her to stop.* But the crescent moon revealed the glint of Star's knife plunging into a blanket-covered man. Thunder heard the last sigh of air leaving his lungs, the only sound in the camp.

It is too late to stop now. Thunder crept to the closest man. Firmly grasping her knife, she aimed it just below the man's voice box. Just as she sliced downward, a flash of lightning lit the camp, and a burst of thunder shook the air. The man reflexively jerked his head. The knife landed just below the jaw, and blood gushed from the wound. The man's piercing scream tore through the stillness.

Terrified, Thunder ran blindly for the river, hearing shouts and gunfire. Her left foot came down on a small rock, twisting her ankle and snapping a tendon. The stabbing pain caused her to limp the last few steps and awkwardly launch herself into the water. She swam, ignoring her throbbing ankle and the bullets pelting the water around her.

Some distance downstream, she emerged from the water unhit and rose to her feet at the river's bank. She cursed herself as she hobbled briskly toward the ravine. *Had I killed the sleeping soldier instantly, the raid might have succeeded.*

Lightning leaped wildly across the northern sky, and sharp claps of thunder reverberated through the air. Finally, she reached the ravine where they had hidden the gelding and the bay. She fell to her knees, thanking Child of the Water for keeping her safe. She pleaded for the spirits to watch over Star and Stormy.

Thunder put on her clothes. While she sat, listening for any signs of Star, a mist began to fall. Worries about her friend hounded her, driving her to self-condemnation. *I forced Star to join in the attack, so I should at least have stayed with her to fight. Why did I run and leave her to face death alone? How could I have been such a coward?* Adding to the chill of her thoughts, the mist grew into a pouring rain.

At last, a sickly yellow dawn bled through the darkness, spreading wan light over the land. Thunder tried to stand, bringing a searing pain to her ankle. She examined it and found it shockingly discolored and swollen. *Serves me right. At least I am being punished for my cowardice.* She decided to look for Star on foot, leaving the horses behind in case she returned. As the sun burst from behind the mottled clouds, she limped her way up a hogback ridge and started downward.

She paused to perform her customary morning prayer and included a request for a sign of her two friends. Thirst brought Thunder shuffling to the river, and she drank greedily. Fear gnawed at her belly, and her soul grew heavy at the thought of losing Star and Stormy. She chastised herself for putting her own quest for vengeance ahead of Star's life. *I owe her an apology. I should have settled for the horses, as she advised.*

Thunder's ankle continued to throb, compounding her misery. If she did not take care of it soon, she would lose her ability to walk. She limped to a nearby stump, sat, and inspected the injury. After drawing out her knife, she pushed the point into the swollen flesh until oily dark blood shot from the puncture.

As she finished bleeding her ankle, a soft nicker filled her heart with joy. Thunder whirled around just in time to see Star cresting the ridge, riding Stormy and leading the other horses. The agonizing tension left Thunder and the fear in her heart disappeared, making her dizzy with joy.

Star rode up to Thunder. "Are you hurt?"

"I am not hurt!" Thunder hissed. "I was sick with worry. Where have you been all night?"

Star laughed as she dismounted. "You sound like a blue jay scolding her young."

Thunder stumbled awkwardly to Star and threw her arms around her. "Oh, Star. I thought I would never see you again." She released the hug and stepped back. "My dear friend, I am so sorry I did not respect your advice to begin with. You are so much wiser and know so much more of the spirits than me. I will never disbelieve you again."

Thunder felt Stormy's warm nose on her neck and heard soft nickering sounds in her ear. She turned and hugged him. He reminded her of life back home, when Grandfather was still alive and Golden Eagle was busily preparing for their lives together. Stormy nuzzled into her as she affectionately stroked his long neck and unkempt mane. "I am so happy you are back with me." She knew those village days were gone but having Stormy—her only living link to her people—would ease her grief.

Thunder turned back to Star. "How did you escape the raid unharmed?"

"I had just removed my blade from a second soldier when your victim screamed," Star said. "I grabbed the dead men's rifles then ran to the corral and donned my clothes. The horses had already panicked and broken loose. Knowing I could not find them in the darkness, I slept under a lovely spruce tree a bowshot from the corral. At daybreak, I walked uphill and found them grazing at the other end of the meadow." She smiled. "I simply motioned and willed them to follow me. When we got back to the corral, I thought the riding gear might have value, so I saddled and bridled all the horses. We moved on and found you."

"You are a true shaman."

Star smiled shyly. "All I do is understand the spirits' wishes and not rebel against them."

Thunder laughed. "If I stay with you long enough, maybe someday I will learn." She grabbed Stormy's reins, mounted, and rode him to the ravine. Star followed on a mare, leading the other horses.

After comparing stories, Thunder concluded two soldiers were still alive. She still felt reluctant to kill the boy needlessly, but she also knew she had unfinished business with them. "I want to go back there," she declared, "and look those soldiers in the eye."

"If you go," Star said with a sigh, "I should go with you."

They saddled the trapper's horses, threw on the supplies, then remounted and started for the soldiers. "With six horses," Star bragged, "I will be considered wealthy when I reach the Cheyenne. I wonder if a girl can provide her own dowry?"

Thunder raised an eyebrow. "You think you will have to buy a husband, do you?"

Star broke into a silly grin, then sobered. "How bad is your foot? Should I take a look at it?"

"Not right now. I have already bled it."

After crossing the river, the girls felt brazen as they galloped across the meadow in plain sight. Returning to the site of the ambush, they saw the young sentry digging graves, and they slowed their horses to a stop just outside the camp.

The sentry's head shot up when he saw them. He threw down his shovel and grabbed his rifle in one swift movement. Then, he seemed to change his mind and smiled.

"Well, I'll be danged if'n it ain't two little Injun gals bringing our horses back. Howdy there, gals!" he yelled. "Have y'all seen the ornery fellers who stole them horses? They killed three of our men." He pointed to the three fresh graves.

A hundred yards away, behind the cover of trees, Sergeant O'Riley overheard Private Casey talking to a savage. He dropped the armful of firewood he'd collected, yanked on his rifle strap, and swung the gun over his head. In an instant, he had his gun cocked with his finger on the trigger. Heart pounding, he hoped against all odds they'd stumbled across the squaw who'd torn his eye.

Peering through the tree leaves, he saw an Injun girl cupping her hands around her mouth. "Wasn't no men!" she yelled. "It was us, Falling Star and me, Talks Like Thunder! We're the ones who took your horses and killed your men!"

O'Riley raised his rifle and looked through the scope with his good eye, catching a glimpse of the silent one. *Better to shoot the loudmouth first. That'll shut her up.* His scope revealed the talker as she called, "Leave this land and our people alone, or we will return for your life!"

Christ Almighty, that's her! She's as good as dead now! He pulled the trigger.

Just then, the girl's horse reared.

Hell! I missed! O'Riley took aim again, but the girl ran the stallion along the riverbank, followed by her companion and five saddled horses.

Three missed shots later, O'Riley flushed with rage. *That's my horse she's riding! I'll tear that little Injun bitch limb from limb!*

"So, there were two men, as we thought," Star said. Not having seen the other soldier troubled her. It felt somehow significant.

"We will let the sentry and the other one be," Thunder said.

"I thought your whole life's mission was to kill soldiers to free the souls of your people."

"These men will suffer enough for me. It will do them good to embarrass themselves returning to the fort on foot."

Finding Stormy must have eased Thunder's thirst for revenge, Star thought. *Hopefully, it has restored her confidence as well.*

"Let us find Golden Eagle," Star said as she looked to the south, seeing brown, barren land below the horizon.

Thunder rubbed Stormy's neck. She seemed to wrestle with the decision, more than Star had anticipated. Then, she turned Stormy south. With an uneasy foreboding, Star likewise turned her mount, and they rode straight into the endless desert wind.

FOURTEEN

New Mexico Territory, July 1879

The high-noon sun roasted the backs of the sentry and his sergeant. Neither man knew how many miles of steep hills they had walked, nor their exact whereabouts.

"By God, I wish I had the chance to kill them savage squaws," Sergeant O'Riley moaned as they approached a heavily forested valley. "Just six weeks back, I bribed the horse keepers two months' wages to have that black stallion assigned to me. Then, that Injun loudmouth rides off with it. Nothing lower than a horse thief." Looking around the wilderness with his good eye, he felt sure them damn redskins were hiding out there somewhere, like scorpions under a rock. In all his years of fighting them, he had learned they always moved, like wolves following game. Their constant roving, more than anything else, made them so damn hard to catch. "If we had our horses," he growled, "we'd've made it to the fort by now."

Private Casey looked him in the eye. "It ain't my fault you got tired and wandered off to get firewood. You're the one that left me to dig them graves alone."

The sergeant ignored Casey's retort. The densely packed pines seemed to close in around him, wrapping him in shadow. "They're a strange people," he told the boy. "They run around here owning only what they carry. They steal what they need from wagon trains, ranchers, and farmers. Those damned savages butcher anyone who has something they want."

The boy replied with little enthusiasm. "I heard some men at the fort say they were gentle with their kin."

"So? If you don't heed what I'm telling ya, you'll learn too late how ferocious they are when seeking revenge."

"Do you think vengeance is what made them two girls attack us?"

"Could be. Some say the women are as fierce as the men."

"If they're so all-fired mean, how come they didn't kill me last night?"

Having no answer, the sergeant fell silent. Seeing the boy's relief that he had stopped lecturing, O'Riley fumed all the more.

Three days and a continual string of profanity later, Sergeant O'Riley stood with blistered feet in Captain Baker's office, delivering his oral report. Barney stood off to the side, his worn brown hat clutched in his hand.

"I'm telling you it was two young Injun gals!" O'Riley bellowed. He could feel his scarred eyelid fluttering and his face swelling with redness. He felt as though blood might spurt through his pores at any moment. "They called themselves Falling Star and Talks Like Thunder."

"Calm down, Sergeant, before you have a stroke," Captain Baker advised. "I believe you. It's just hard to understand how two girls could kill three men, steal five horses, and leave you walking sixty miles."

"Weren't humans, Cap'n," Barney broke in, showing a couple of missing front teeth. "Musta been them haints they're always dancin' up."

"Shut up, Barney. I don't want to hear any more of that ridiculous talk around here. The new recruits are scared enough. If they get wind of ghost warriors, they'll likely try to run home to their mamas."

"Ain't like me and the boy is gonna spill the beans," O'Riley whined.

"Barney, find Sergeant Clark and bring him here. I hope he's capable of catching those girls."

Barney saluted and walked out.

Alone with the captain, O'Riley stood aghast. "You know we ain't proud of being took by them gals. But give me another chance."

Captain Baker's annoyance erupted into anger. "Well, Sergeant," he said, picking up a bunch of papers from his desk. "First, I dealt with Private Wilkensen's complaint of your misconduct with an Indian girl. I never bought your story that Wilkensen forced your wagonload of girls off the road. When he demanded you unshackle the girl, and you refused, he knifed you in the eye. With your accounts at odds, the tribunal only issued a warning."

O'Riley's brain felt numb, unable to function. *That bastard, Jim and his Christian morality. After all, she was just a little squaw. Why would he care?*

"Then," Captain Baker continued, "rumors circulated around here about another matter. It seems you and your men massacred every man, woman, and child of fifty or so Apache escapees. Your orders were simply to bring them back to the reservation."

O'Riley opened his mouth to speak, but Baker roared, "Don't even try to tell me you couldn't find them! Believe me, if I'd sent out a platoon and found evidence, I'd have locked you up for life! However, it was impossible with my troops stretched so thin. After all that, I gave you four men and a simple patrol assignment."

O'Riley felt the blood rising to his face again. *Why, I should be decorated for killing off them damn redskins!* His heart pounded, threatening to explode. *Those trappers meeting us on our way back, and switching the Injuns' weapons and trinkets for cash saved my hide.*

"Now," Baker concluded, "after this rotation, you've lost three of your men to two Indian girls. Sergeant, you've exhausted all my patience." The captain shoved the papers into O'Riley's chest. "I order you to leave for Fort Tharp within the hour, carrying these records, and report to Colonel Edwards. You will be at his mercy."

O'Riley took the papers, saluted, and walked out, dumbfounded. *I'm the best redskin killer Baker has! It's that damned Injun bitch, Talks Like Thunder, who ruined my life. Somehow, I'll find my way back to these parts just to kill her. By God, it'll be worth it.*

FIFTEEN

New Mexico Territory, August 1879

Thunder and Star had ridden south for a half moon in search of Golden Eagle. Upon reaching the reservation that Thunder had escaped six moons earlier, they found it empty. No lodges remained, only abandoned shells of agency buildings. *Good that Golden Eagle is not here,* Thunder thought. *I do not want to face him.*

The girls set out along a trail leading southeastward, in the direction the soldiers had taken Golden Eagle.

At nightfall, they reached a broad river, the one the Mexicans called the Rio Grande. They camped on the bank for the night, crossed the river the next morning, and continued down the path. In the early afternoon, they came to a newly constructed fort. Leaving the horses a safe distance away, the girls went to take a closer look. After concealing themselves behind small shrubs, they observed the compound throughout the afternoon. Soldiers moved in and out of buildings. Others unloaded an arriving wagon train, then fed and watered the horses.

At sundown, Star said, "Golden Eagle and the other warriors must have finished the fort and been taken elsewhere."

"I have no idea where he could be now," Thunder said without looking at her. "I can kill soldiers while I help you find the Cheyenne, so let us return north."

Star sighed. "You should not give up looking for Golden Eagle. It would be best if I am with you when you meet him, but I will respect your wishes."

She does not understand, Thunder thought. *Her intentions are good, but I do not want to face Golden Eagle again, soiled as I am.*

The next morning, the girls started back north, following a little-used trail. At midday, seeking rest and a meal, they steered their herd of horses up a mountain and sheltered among a cluster of boulders. Beyond them lay a tiny spring-fed pool. A rocky incline rose to one side, and a trickle of water flowed out from its opposite end.

The girls removed the gear, and the horses trotted to the pool and drank. Their waterskins in hand, Star and Thunder found a shaded rock and sat. Star took a long drink, but Thunder only stared at the ground.

"You seem preoccupied, sister. Is something bothering you?"

"I suppose I am just relieved we did not find Golden Eagle. How can I convince him I did nothing wrong when I cannot even convince myself?" She sighed, looked up, and held Star's gaze.

"Are you ready to examine that day again and be honest with yourself about it?" Star asked.

"Yes, I think I can do that."

"It takes time to grow strong enough to relive such moments. If you feel you are ready, I will help you."

"Relive?" Thunder said hesitantly. "I do not know…I prefer not to relive that day, but I suppose I need to."

"I believe you are strong enough. Just now, for the first time, you did not avert your eyes when we talked about the attack. Your heart will tell you if you are not ready."

Star walked toward the water, which the horses had abandoned. She gestured for Thunder to follow, saying, "Tie your braids together behind your head."

The horses had left the pool only half full, but its reflective surface had grown smooth again. "Sit at the water's edge," Star directed, "and look into the pool until you see your face."

Reluctantly, Thunder seated herself by the pool, leaned over it, and gazed downward.

"Look into your eyes," Star said.

Wrestling with her apprehension, Thunder concentrated on Star's instructions. Slowly she felt her body relax, and her breath fell into a deep, slow rhythm. She looked down at her reflected face, then into her eyes, focusing on each dark pupil. *A part of me so empty, emotionless, and pure.*

"Think back to the day of the attack," Star instructed. "You were inspecting your snares, and you came to the last one. Something unusual happened there. Something distracted you from noticing the trapper's presence. What was it?"

The vivid scene erupted in Thunder's mind. "I found a weasel in the small snare, caught by its hindquarters." She heard herself speaking in a quiet, calm voice, as if from a great distance away. "It twisted back and forth as far as the rope would let it, trying to free itself." Thunder shuddered from deep within, afraid she was drifting into a realm beyond her control, but she took another breath and continued remembering.

"When the weasel saw me, its eyes locked onto mine, bared its teeth, and snarled ferociously. The animal was under a huge tree. I felt the wind blowing on my left side, and the tree was slightly behind me to my right. I put all my focus into striking accurately with my club. The moment I killed the animal, I blacked out... I awoke under the white man and started struggling, and I felt a knife at my throat." Thunder flung her arms up.

"Relax, Thunder," Star said soothingly. "We are both observers now. Look back into the pool."

Thunder looked into the centers of her eyes, her alarm fading back into calm detachment. "I do not remember how long I held off his knife before you killed him."

"Thunder," Star said, "slowly bring yourself back to the present."

Thunder sat silent, contemplating. "I was only distracted for a moment."

"It is very unlikely the trapper got there at that exact moment. I believe he saw the weasel in your trap, hid behind the tree, and waited for you. He expected you to give your full attention to dealing with the weasel, and he attacked at that moment. Regardless of warrior training, no one can pay full attention to every unlikely threat. Besides, you would have needed eyes in the back of your head to know the trapper crept behind you. That is why warriors do not go into enemy territory alone."

Thunder nodded, surprised by the feeling of relief washing over her.

"You did not bring this violation upon yourself. You punish yourself unjustly. Understand that I am also responsible for your defilement, for not checking the snares with you. Do not blame yourself. You did nothing wrong, and I am deeply sorry."

Thunder gazed down at the water again, and for the first time, she saw herself truly. She beheld an Apache warrior, and also a maiden wrongfully deprived of her innocence. She suffered from a grave injury, but she would heal. She bore no more blame than did the smooth, gray pebbles at the bottom of the pool.

Sometime later, Thunder approached Star, who sat among the boulders. "I want to throw out everything belonging to the trapper, except the guns."

"I suppose we can do as you wish, but we should keep the trapper's horses, riding gear, and what is left of the food."

"Yes, we will need the horses and gear, but I hate the trapper's food. I will not eat any more."

"I hated it too. But it is foolish to throw food away in the desert."

"It won't hurt us to go hungry for a few sleeps."

Star sighed. "All right. If you must throw it away," she said empathetically, "let us get started."

Together, they tossed out the trapper's buffalo skins, burlap bags, food, and blankets. Seeing the tainted goods scattered around camp, Thunder relaxed. "I feel better now." She untied her braids and ran her fingers through her hair until it freely fell to her shoulders. The ugly reminders out of her possession, Thunder slowly began to feel more like herself.

After they walked back to the boulders, Star pulled out two pemmican pouches from the gear and handed one to Thunder, who sat and ate until she emptied the pouch. She got up, intending to load the packhorse with their few remaining supplies, but when glancing northeast, she noticed a distant movement. Raising her hand to shield her eyes from the early afternoon sun, she saw wisps of dust rising from the landscape. She told Star to bring the rifles, and they ducked behind a boulder overlooking the northern edge of the plateau.

A small caravan drew close enough for Thunder to hear the clop-clop-clop of fast-trotting horses, accompanied by the smooth roll of metal-rimmed wheels grinding against mountain stone. She watched as the procession wound its way down a serpentine trail.

A lean, brown-skinned man of about fifty winters walked in front of the others. Taller than most Mexicans, he wore a look of suffering on his face.

A small, sure-footed burro came next, carrying a hawk-faced boy of about sixteen winters. The burro wore a bell fastened to a rope around its neck. Thunder chuckled, wondering if the tinkling sound was to announce the traders' arrival. She could not determine whether the Mexicans were brave or just plain stupid. After all, they were traveling through Apache territory.

Thunder felt a twinge of pity for the boy. He wore ragged brown pantaloons, gathered around his middle and hitched up with a piece of grass rope. His overly large white shirt, dirt-streaked and wet with sweat, sagged on his thin frame. A hot wind blew relentlessly across the dry earth, swirling dust around the burro's hooves. The animal so runty that the boy's feet almost dragged on the ground.

A covered wooden wagon passed next. The driver, an older, fat man, wore a mustache that reminded Thunder of a shock of bunch-grass hanging upside down to dry. He rocked along the rough road, singing drunkenly about a *señorita* in Laredo, and stopped to curse a long-armed saguaro reaching out to claw him.

Behind the wagon, two horsemen rode single file down the trail.

When the travelers reached the base of the mountain, the driver stopped singing and shouted, *"¡Alto, alto!"* He slid from the seat with surprising agility. After unhooking the harness, he clouted the mule on the rump, and growled, *"Arre, mula."* Freed of its burden, the grateful beast broke into a shambling half-trot, then lay down and rolled in the dust.

The two cowpokes followed the driver's lead and dismounted as well. One unsaddled the horses, and the other disappeared into the canvas-covered wagon.

Thunder turned to Star, finding her eyes rivetted on the Mexicans. "What do you think?"

"Too many to waste bullets on if we do not have to."

The man in the wagon brought out a girl of about their age and a woman with some forty winters. He pushed the woman hard, causing her to sprawl on the ground.

"¡Quita tus manos de ella, cabròn!" the girl shouted.

"Chinga tu madre," the man said, striking the girl.

He turned his back, and the girl jumped him from behind, throwing him off balance. *"Pinche viejo,"* she cursed, telling the man again to leave her mother alone.

He threw her to the ground and shouted, *"¡No tienes que decirme lo que tengo que hacer! ¡Ándale, quiero comer!"* He turned and buried his pointy-toed boot in the mother's back.

"Pinche viejo, pendejo," Thunder swore under her breath. She picked up her rifle and took aim. "I am going to kill that son of a she-dog."

"No," Star whispered, pushing down the gun barrel. "I have a plan."

Thunder reluctantly agreed to retreat into deeper cover.

Back near the pool, Star told Thunder, "To free the women, we will need to be weaponless to keep the trader and cowpokes from becoming suspicious." She started etching a map in the sand. "First, I need to know if the boy and the old man will try to stop us."

"Since they have no weapons, they must be captives too and will be glad to be free."

"Why haven't they escaped?"

"If they ran off, the trader and his men would easily catch them on horses. Even if they did get away, they would no doubt die crossing the desert on foot."

"Knowing that makes my plan easy." Star drew an arc. "We will leave our five other horses here and ride to the crest of the mountain. After circling around the ridge," Star said, pointing to it, "we will ride down to the Mexicans, and lure them to later follow us up the mountain. Once we leave their sight, we can return here and watch them from the ridge."

They waited until the sun dropped below the horizon, turning the clear blue sky to a muddy gray. Thunder mounted Stormy and scratched the space between his ears. The noble animal responded by snorting with pleasure. She and Star rode nonchalantly down the precipice, making enough noise to alert the Mexicans of their approach. Startled merchants were known to shoot Indians without hesitation.

Gathered around a campfire, the peddler and cowboys laughed and passed around an earthen jug, taking long draughts from it. The aromatic scent of chili hung in the air, making Thunder's stomach growl.

"¡Música, música!" the boss man shouted. The boy picked up his guitar and started playing. The men sang loudly and off-key. The old man's eyes kept darting toward the wagon where the woman and the girl were tied.

Thunder tried to remain calm. It was difficult, though, since she carried no weapon. "I must be crazy," she mumbled, "for listening to you."

"Quiet," Star hissed.

When they had drawn close enough to be heard, Thunder called, *"¡Hola, amigos!"*

"¡Bienvenidas!" said the *gordo*, the welcome in his eyes as well as on his meaty lips.

Thunder stopped but made no move to dismount. Star positioned herself alongside.

"Buenas noches. ¿Qué honor que me visiten?"

"What did he say?" Star whispered nervously.

"He asked why we honor him with a visit," Thunder said before turning back to the *gordo*. *"¿Tienes licor?"* Taking his silence in stride, she went on to explain that her father had seen them making camp and wondered if they had liquor to sell. She pointed to the top of the ridge to show the Mexicans her father's supposed location.

"¿Por qué su padre envía solas a sus queridas hijas de noche?"

Thunder could see he was suspicious. *"No, señor, no estamos solas, mi padre tiene muchos soldados, pero están cansados y necesitan descansar."*

Star whispered, "What are—?"

Thunder shot her a glare. "Hush!"

"Sí, señorita, but I do not have the white man's whiskey," the *gordo* answered in mixed English. "I only have a Mexican drink called *pulque*. What does your father have to trade?"

Thunder blinked, surprised he knew English, but followed his lead. "*Mi padre* has many fine horses, and silver too."

"*Bueno. ¿Cuánto pulque por el caballo?*"

"*No, señor, el caballo es mío y no lo cambio.*"

"What is he saying now?" Star asked.

"He said he does not have whiskey, only *pulque*."

"What is that?"

"It is an alcohol drink made from cactus, much like the *tiswin* we make. He also asked me how much I wanted for Stormy, and I told him Stormy was mine and not for sale. And if you do not stop asking so many questions, I will never finish."

"If you do not wish to sell your horse," the trader cut in, "then where is the horse your father wants to trade?"

"My father has many fine horses," Thunder snapped impatiently. "He sent us to ask if you want to trade, but you must speak to him to make the terms."

"Bring your father and his horses in the morning, and we will talk."

"*Perdón, señor,* my father waits now. He wishes to drink tonight, not tomorrow." Thunder bowed politely from her waist. She had learned at the school that such a gesture showed respect, although she felt no respect for this fat drunkard. She pretended only to win his confidence. "We must go. My father awaits your answer."

"Tell your *papá* we will come when we finish our evening meal."

"*Muchas gracias, señor,*" Thunder said as she turned her horse to leave.

"*Adios, muchachas,*" the smiling boy called after them.

As the two girls rode up the rocky incline, Thunder laughed. "We should not try that again. I need to start teaching you Spanish, and English too."

Star giggled. "You probably should."

After reaching cover, they circled back to camp as planned, and soon, as Star had predicted, they heard the trader and his men ride up the mountain. The girls crawled to the ridge and looked below. Each rider carried a rifle and pistol within reach, and the trader rode the mule with a keg strapped behind his saddle. When they disappeared, Thunder and Star returned to their hideout. They saddled the other five horses, mounted their own, and led them to the Mexicans' camp.

The moment the girls rode in, the old man and the boy rose to their feet. Seeing the glint of Thunder's gun in the moonlight, they raised their hands in surrender.

"Corta las cuerdas," she ordered, using her rifle to point at the women and giving the man her knife.

"Sí, señorita." The old man walked to the tied captives and cut the ropes.

The woman and the girl humbly walked toward Thunder, rubbing their wrists. Thunder smiled at them, then directed her words to the old man and the boy. *"Amigos,* you may leave by yourselves or come with us. It is your choice."

They conversed in rapid-fire Spanish, unintelligible to Thunder. *"Señoritas,* you are very kind," the old man said, returning the knife to Thunder. "We would like to go with you for now, then separate at a safe distance from here. I must return this young gentleman to his family."

"It is agreed if you help us now." Thunder smiled and slid off Stormy's back.

Everyone ransacked the supplies, scouring them for food and

water. After loading what they wanted, they threw everything else in a pile under the wagon. The old man sprinkled it with lamp oil, topping it with a burning log from the fire.

Star separated two mares from the others, led them to the woman and the girl and offered them each a pair of reins, and they accepted gratefully. The old man and boy smiled when taking the last two horses.

Everyone mounted and rode deeper into the desert.

SIXTEEN

New Mexico Territory, August 1879

"Do you see anyone, José?"

"No, *señor*." José swung around to face his boss. "*¡Ay, ay, ay!* Look behind you. There is fire on the desert!"

"Holy Mother, it's our camp!" Sanchez shouted. *"¡Ándale! ¡Ándale! ¡Apúrate!"* he screamed, beating the mule's backside with his puffy hand. On the way down, he repeatedly cursed at his men for losing his trade goods and captives.

When they reached camp, nothing remained but glowing coals and the iron wheel-rims of the wagon. These lay atop the smoldering ashes, warped grotesquely by the intense heat.

"*¡Pendejos!* We were fools to believe those Indians," Sanchez whined. "There were no Apaches waiting up there."

"In the morning, we will find the little savages," José promised. "Won't we, Paco?"

Paco was pissed and didn't say anything. *The gordo keeps saying "we" are stupid, when "we" didn't have a damned thing to do with his decision. It was his idea to go traipsing up there at night. He's so greedy, he'd sell his own mother if he got the chance!*

Paco refilled the jug from the keg of *pulque* and sat beside José near the burnt-out wagon. After taking a long swig, he rubbed his mouth against his dirty shirtsleeve, then passed the jug to José.

At daybreak, the three hungover Mexicans rode away from their burnt-out camp. They quickly picked up the trail but lost it before mid-morning.

Giving up on finding the girls, they turned north. Sanchez hoped his animals would last long enough to reach the waterhole in Mescalero territory by day's end.

"I have crossed this desert many times," Paco said, "but never without food and water. Do you think we should go on with nothing but this *pulque*?"

José rolled his eyes, then retorted with irritation, "What other choice do we have?"

"Now, *compadres*," Sanchez broke in, "let's not get all sideways. We all know there's nothing behind us. We have no choice; all we can do is keep moving."

José and Paco nodded reluctantly.

Before long, the hot wind wrung every drop of moisture from their bodies, and they began sipping from the jug to quench their thirst. By mid-afternoon, they still could not find any trace of the rapscallion girls. In fact, they were so drunk they didn't bother to relieve themselves properly. Soon, a caustic odor rose in puffs as their wet pants crunched rhythmically against the leather saddles.

As they rode, Sanchez whined constantly about his hatred for the *Apachería*, the vast expanse of sandy soil around them. In this enormous wasteland, dotted with cacti and an occasional stunted mesquite tree, only the hardiest creatures could survive.

Late that afternoon, he spotted a cavalry unit making camp next to the watering hole he had been searching for. The *pulque*, long finished, had left him sick, sober, and hungry. Desperately needing the soldiers' help, he rode in.

Sanchez noticed a sergeant cautiously take a few steps toward them. He and his men raised their hands and moved their mounts slowly ahead. Upon reaching the soldier, they dismounted. As Sanchez introduced himself, he saw the sergeant wrinkle his nose, reminding him of the dampness of his pants. He smelled of urine.

The man called himself Sergeant Clark, and he and Sanchez shook hands. The sergeant wiped his hand on his pants, and said he was looking for two young Indian girls causing trouble.

Sanchez frowned, wishing he'd had the chance to clean up. "*Sí, señor*, we have seen those savage sisters. We too are trying to catch them. They stole my servants and burned my wagon of trade goods!" Enraged by the memory, Sanchez couldn't stop himself from shaking his fat, stubby finger in Clark's face.

The sergeant turned toward his men and said in a raised voice, "This man saw the same girls who killed O'Riley's men and stole his horses. I'd bet my last bullet on it!" He turned back toward Sanchez, then asked more quietly, "Was one of them riding a big black stallion?"

"*Sí*. She is a loud talker, and the other one stays quiet."

"That's them, all right," Clark said in a grimly satisfied tone. After a moment, he asked, "How far behind them do you think we are?"

"*Dos días,*" Sanchez said. The sergeant's face wore a look of puzzlement, obviously having no idea what he had just said. *Stupid gringo.* Sanchez smirked, then said, "Two days."

Clark wrinkled his nose again. "We will camp here tonight and start again at daybreak, if you want to ride with us."

Sanchez hesitated, thinking about his empty stomach before replying. "If you are in need of our help, we will go with you. If not, we would rather wait at the fort."

"Don't worry, we won't need help. We can catch the whole kit and caboodle of 'em by ourselves. I'll bring 'em to the fort dead or alive, makes me no difference."

"A word of caution, Sergeant. You and your men best watch your backs. The Mescaleros around here are the deadliest in the whole Apache nation. I know them well; my people have been fighting them for years."

Sanchez saw the irritation on Clark's face but continued with his lecture. "All Apaches are dangerous, but these Mescaleros are treacherous."

"Thanks for the warning." Clark smirked. "I think we can handle those little girls all right."

"My people claim the Apache are harder to catch than an eagle." Sanchez smiled slyly, realizing he had touched a sore spot in Clark's self-confidence. "If you could spare a little food, we'll be on our way." He could tell the sergeant didn't like him or his advice, and he didn't much care. He wanted his servants back and his stomach full, so he said no more.

The Mexicans took their horses to the waterhole, and all drank their fill. They washed up, rinsed out their *pulque* keg, and filled it with water. After finishing their meal, the soldiers gave them directions and supplies. Clark and Sanchez wished each other luck.

Sanchez mounted, swung his mule north, and gestured for his companions to follow. *The sergeant is a very foolish man to laugh at my warning. I hope he will still be laughing when he finds those girls.*

Paco and José listened while Sanchez translated his conversation with the soldiers. "He swears they will catch those thieving *putas*. He also said if we ride for two nights, we can reach the fort about sunup the day after tomorrow."

As the Mexicans rode away, Sergeant Clark told his men, "Sanchez called those girls savage sisters. He sure named 'em right, didn't he?" Clark gazed across the wasteland. Aside from bunchgrass and rolling tumbleweed, he saw nothing except sand and shale. "Another sandy camp," he grumbled. "God, I don't know which I hate more: them damned Apaches or another sleepless night slapping sand gnats."

A Tonkawa scout standing nearby heard the sergeant's complaint and turned his face to hide his grin. His people had hunted Apaches for years, and he knew they could survive almost anything. A Mescalero could wear out his toughest enemy. Even their women could walk across a burning desert or climb the face of a barren range with stealth and speed. In brush and mountainous territory, Mescaleros could travel farther and faster on foot than most soldiers could on horses. An average Mescalero could survive for days with no food or water. They were not like these pampered soldier boys who needed tents to sleep in and hot meals twice a day.

No, the scout thought, *the soldiers should not underestimate the Apaches.* He had studied the habits and behavior of those swift, wiry people. Their war parties often journeyed hundreds of miles into Texas and Mexico in order to display their bravery and obtain wealth. *No, no, Sergeant, you are foolish to make light of your enemies just because they are female. But it is not my job to teach you babies how to fight. I am paid to track.*

It was only his own hide he wanted to save, and he vowed to do that.

SEVENTEEN

New Mexico Territory, August 1879

Thunder's group traveled through the night in silence, fearing the trader would pursue them. Finally, when Thunder felt safe, they stopped to sleep. As they unpacked their gear in the moonlight, Thunder introduced herself and Star in Spanish. The old man nodded in acknowledgment and gave his own name as Oscar. Then he introduced the other Mexicans: the woman, Victoria; her daughter, Maria; and the young boy, Roberto.

The group awoke at sunrise. They all mounted and started the day's travel. Oscar steered his horse next to Thunder's and rode silently alongside her. When Thunder felt unsure of which way to go, Oscar offered direction with certainty, proving his competence as a guide.

"Oscar," Thunder said, "keep us ahead of the trader and close to water. In this heat, we will not last long without it." He turned south, leading them straight into the bowels of the desert.

Victoria and Maria did not speak unless spoken to. They accepted food and water when offered but asked for nothing. Thunder noticed how well both women handled their horses and how they rode without complaint through the burning heat.

"Buenas soldaderas," Thunder told Victoria, who smiled at the compliment.

In a low voice, Oscar suggested Thunder not grow too friendly with her new companions. The white men's killing and plundering of so many villages, he explained, had made the Mescaleros even deadlier than before.

"If a war party should find us," he said, "they will probably kill all but you. Being Apache, your life might be spared unless you try to protect us."

Oscar's thinking took Thunder aback. *He is willing to sacrifice his life and all the others, so I can make a deal with raiding warriors.*

"Oscar," Thunder assured him, "I betray no one who travels with me. If raiders attack us, I expect all of us to unite and fight off our enemy."

The old man's eyes widened in surprise; then he nodded in understanding. Relaxing slightly, he began telling the story of his and Roberto's capture.

"The boy's grandfather, *Señor* Roberto Carlos Coronado, is a wealthy and influential man. For nearly my whole life, I worked for the elder Roberto at his ranch, a half-day's ride south of the Rio Grande. A month ago, we were traveling to El Paso when

Mescaleros raided our caravan and took me and the boy. We lived in the Mescalero village until two weeks ago, when Sanchez came to peddle his wares. The Indians sold me and Roberto to Sanchez for seven horses. One night, I overheard the drunken cowpokes talk about their plan for us. Sanchez had heard stories about an affluent young boy kidnapped by Mescaleros. He had bought Roberto, hoping to extract a large ransom from the boy's family. He purchased me as well, to serve as a liaison to the Coronados."

Oscar took a deep breath. "I could find my way back to the well-guarded *ranchero*. I would have tried to escape before, but I dared not risk the boy's life. The section of desert we must cross is very dangerous. If you could help me get the boy home, *Señor* Coronado would reward you with gold."

"I have no need for gold. Besides, I promised Star I would help her find the Cheyenne."

"If you do not want gold, *Señor* Coronado might give you one of his Mescalero Apache laborers in trade."

Walks Alone was a Mescalero, she thought, recalling how the whites forced her to stay at the school. Could she rescue another Apache from that? *If I free a Mescalero warrior, he might agree to help me kill soldiers!* She calmed herself and said flatly, "I will speak to Star about it."

After they had made camp and finished the evening meal, Thunder excitedly told Star all she had learned from Oscar. She included his request for their help.

"Did you agree?" Star asked.

"I told him I had to talk to you."

"You know I am eager to find the Cheyenne and travel to Grandmother's Land."

Thunder felt a twinge of disappointment. "I suppose that was not the answer I was hoping for."

"You want to help them?"

Thunder hesitated a moment before answering. "I have been thinking. I would have starved among the White Mountain Apaches, but my grandfather came for me and saved my life. He gave me a family when I had no other. That is why I want to return Roberto to his family."

"It is compassionate of you to want to help the boy and free the Apache."

"Yes, but it is another five suns' ride southeast. But what about you? Is it all right with you?"

"This sounds dangerous, and it will take both of us away from our missions." After a moment of silence, Star reached out, clasped Thunder's arm, and smiled. "I think it is worth it, though. But what about finding Golden Eagle?"

Thunder frowned. "We can think about that after we deliver the boy."

On the sixth morning after fleeing from Sanchez, the motley group had crossed the Rio Grande and entered Mexico. Before long, they saw isolated villages in the distance. When Oscar saw a group of adobe buildings or a herd of sheep, he quickly led the group away, explaining *bandidos* might recognize Roberto and try to capture him again.

Before midday, they crested a hill and saw the ranch. A sprawl of low adobe buildings with roofs of weathered red tiles lay before them. Pink and purple bougainvillea crowned the glistening white walls. Their blossoms, tangled among brilliant green leaves, pleased the eye. Thorny vines had grown over the garden walls, providing a soft contrast to the harsh landscape surrounding them. From this distance, they could see a walled garden filled with corn, beans, and other vegetables. Beside it lay a patio with a large, square multi-tiered fountain in the center. Bubbling water glistened as it flowed down the ornamental tiles. White iron benches and pots of colorful flowers made the patio look inviting.

At the ranch's center was a mansion of Spanish design, its long veranda bedecked with elegant marble arches. Thunder could barely see the elaborately carved doors, nestled in a shadowed overhang. On the left side of the villa, upper windows opened to a balcony overlooking a small terrace of freshly strewn white gravel. Roberto Carlos Coronado was indeed a very wealthy man.

Thunder repeated her instructions to Oscar one last time, making certain he understood the trade arrangements. "Be sure he under-stands we are not of the tribe who took his grandson. We have only freed him and brought him home. We want no gold. All we want is an Apache worker. Tell him when the Apache reaches us unharmed, we will send Roberto to him. We will also give him Maria and Victoria."

"*No, por favor, Señorita* Thunder," Victoria protested. "My daughter and I do not belong to these people. We do not want to be slaves again."

"But where will you go?"

"We would like to ride north with you and Star. We are tired of being passed from one man to another. Maria and I will work hard to make ourselves worthy companions."

Thunder thought for a moment and nodded. "It is settled, then," she told Oscar. "We will trade only you and Roberto."

The old man walked swiftly down the slope, his freedom adding a new vigor to his steps. When he neared the hacienda, the field hands laid down their hoes and ran to greet him. To Thunder's relief, three of them ushered him into the main house as though he were a very important person.

Thunder's band grew hot as the sun neared its apex. During the long wait, Thunder counted twenty armed men guarding the property, which made her nervous enough to consider leaving. At last, the front door opened, and Oscar strode out with an older man, a small boy, and two women, one of whom looked middle-aged, the other elderly.

The group walked across the courtyard, Oscar helping the older man—*Señor* Coronado, Thunder guessed. Suddenly, the boy broke loose from the younger woman and ran up the hillside toward her group. Coronado shouted something, and the three field hands emerged from the stables, leading a mule loaded with a water keg, packs, and three rifles.

Thunder watched the Coronados closely. She saw no hidden weapons but kept hers ready just in case.

When the small boy reached them at the top of the hill, he ran to Roberto's open arms. *"Jeremías, mi hermano, te echábamos de menos,"* Roberto cried out, swinging his brother in the air.

As the family grew close enough to hear, *Señor* Coronado called for permission to parley. Thunder motioned him forward, whispering to the others to beware of treachery. Roberto smiled and assured her that his grandfather was a man of honor, and she had no need to distrust him. He would not deceive them or do anything to put his grandsons or himself at risk.

The family continued to approach, the three workers with the mule barely behind them. The Coronados halted, but the workers kept moving.

Thunder was puzzled three men appeared to be part of the trade after she had agreed to one. She smiled in gratitude, then nudged Roberto, motioning for him and Jeremías to go. Roberto ran straight to his grandfather, who gave him a hug and passed him to the others.

"Many thanks for my grandson," the old woman called in Spanish, wiping tears from her cinnamon-colored cheeks.

"Sí, muchas gracias," the grandfather cried, then added, "I am giving you three Mescaleros and a mule with food and water."

"Vaya con Dios," the younger woman said, making the sign of a cross on her chest.

As the Coronados walked back to the ranchero, Star asked, "Who was the other little boy?"

"Jeremías is Roberto's little brother," Thunder said as the three men, wearing brown laborers' clothes and shoes, joined them in silence. Then she translated the rest of the exchange.

"Thank you for setting us free," the oldest man said. "My name is Yellow Dog. My friends, Turtle and Bear Claw, and I are eager to aid you in your journey."

Thunder greeted them, *"Ya-ta-hey,"* then introduced herself,

Falling Star, and the others. "You may ride our horses," she offered, pointing to them.

Each man chose a horse and mounted, with Turtle making room for himself on the horse with the pack frame.

Star swung her reins. "Let us go before these good people have a change of heart."

EIGHTEEN

Mexico, August 1879

The group rode without speaking, for nothing could be heard over the heavy drumming of their horses' hooves. *Señor* Coronado appeared to be a man of honor, as Roberto had said, but Thunder preferred not to take chances. Nevertheless, when she saw the other horses blowing slime, she knew they had to slow down. If they ran any longer, the desert heat would burst their hearts. Stormy showed no sign of distress, having lived his entire life on the western desert. The soldiers' horses, however, unaccustomed to severe heat, could go no farther at this pace without dire risk.

At sundown, they crossed the Rio Grande. Thunder knew this would be their last place to camp with ample water. "We will eat and rest here," she informed the group, "then ride again in the coolness of the moonlight."

The others agreed and dismounted. Thunder gathered wood nearby and started a fire. The Mescaleros rubbed the oily perspiration from the horses, while Victoria and Maria unloaded the packs.

Victoria excitedly discovered a wonderful selection of food and a bag of salt. Maria, busily searching the smaller packs, squealed in delight, "There's coffee, beans, dried chilies, and *masa*!" Both began chopping and slicing with a flurry of energy.

"*Sí, mi'ja, Señor* Coronado has been very generous." Victoria went on humming happily; even the intense heat could not stifle her joy. "I am free! Free as the wind blows. Free of everything and everyone for the first time in many years."

Thunder smiled at the exuberance of the pair. Curious about the Mescaleros, she walked to them and asked about their tribe. While grooming the horses, they talked excitedly at the prospect of seeing their people again. For many seasons they had labored on the ranch, and all agreed *Señor* Coronado had been a kind and generous *patrón*. He had never beaten them, and they had always received adequate food and clothing. Loneliness had been their only complaint. They missed their families and friends and were thankful to be going home.

"How did you become laborers?" Thunder bluntly asked.

"Our village is in the Sacramento Mountains," Yellow Dog responded. "We went to Santa Fe to trade our mescal, and along the way, a large band of Comancheros captured us." He continued brushing around the horse's back where the saddle had rested.

"Later, they sold us to *Señor* Coronado to work in his vegetable garden." Yellow Dog paused and looked Thunder in the eye. "Why did you ask for us in trade?"

"Well, I only asked for one Apache," Thunder replied, petting

Stormy. "But Coronado released all three of you. Also, I was sent to a white-eyes' school two winters ago, where I became friends with a Mescalero named Walks Alone. She was the toughest, most unrelenting person I have ever met. The whites killed her because she would not bend to their ways. I want such strong-willed warriors to help us in this dangerous land."

Yellow Dog nodded, apparently satisfied.

"Do you know where we are now?" Thunder asked as Victoria joined them.

Yellow Dog began speaking in Spanish as a courtesy to Victoria. "I know our village is to the north, but I have never traveled this part of the desert before."

"We came here from the northwest," Thunder said, patting Stormy's nose. "The land north of here is unknown to us too. Should we just go that way until we find your village?"

Yellow Dog wrinkled his brow, then nodded slowly. His apparent uncertainty caused Thunder a moment of unease, but she dismissed it.

"My home was on the western side of the mountains. I am a Three Hills Chiricahua," Thunder added with pride. "Falling Star is Cheyenne. Her village, like mine, was destroyed. Victoria and Maria are far from their home in Mexico."

"You can come with us," Yellow Dog said. "Our village would welcome such fine women."

"Thank you for the invitation, but Star must find the Cheyenne. When she reaches her people safely, the rest of us may return here and accept your offer."

"You will be gladly received at any time."

Victoria smiled, then turned to Thunder. "Do you know where *Señorita* Star is?"

"She is probably searching for medicine plants."

"How can she know the way of medicine?" Yellow Dog asked. "She is only a girl."

"She is a very capable healer," Thunder assured him. "I have seen her heal the broken wing of a red-tailed hawk, and many four-legged animals too."

Maria interrupted the conversation by announcing the food was ready. She did not need to tell them twice. Just then, Star appeared with a basket full of roots and leaves.

They all ate like starving wolves. Thunder could not get enough tortillas and frijoles. But when Star tasted the salsa, she spat it out, yelling, "Aaaah!" Everyone laughed and kept eating.

After filling the keg and their canteens to the brim, the band mounted up and rode. No wind blew that night under the clear sky. The North Star guided them toward where they hoped to find the Mescalero village. They heard no sound in the desert save the relentless *rat-tat-tat* of hooves on the dry sand.

By first light, Thunder had seen no landmarks in the vast, pathless desert. She had no way to measure their progress. In every direction, all she saw was sand, rock, and brush. She glanced back, reassured by their trail. *At least we can turn around and follow our tracks back to the river, if we must.*

The exhausted group halted shortly after sunrise. They refilled their waterskins from the keg, then watered the horses. Thunder sat next to Victoria and asked her about her family.

Victoria sat in silence, staring to the horizon, before finally saying,

"Many years ago, my husband, Pedro, I, and Maria—four years old then—were on our way to the Sunday mass in Galeana, when we were attacked by *bandidos*. They killed Pedro and took Maria and me as slaves. From that time on, we have been passed from one group to another until Sanchez bought us three months ago. I doubt Maria would remember my mother, an elderly woman by now. However, my siblings and friends have children that Maria could share her life with if we ever return home. She would have a good life there."

Thunder nodded. "Life is empty without family. I hope you reunite with them soon."

The two women lay down and rested with the others, sleeping in the sun until they were awakened by a brisk wind that swiftly raised a cloud of fine sand. Before long, dust blotted out the sun, and no one could see anything. Barely able to breathe, they felt around in the packs until they found enough pieces of cloth for everyone to use as face coverings. They lay with their backs to the wind and waited out the storm. By late afternoon, the wind had lessened, allowing the sun to penetrate the dust.

When Thunder saw their tracks had vanished, a sinking feeling flickered in the pit of her stomach. The bad sign compelled her to reconsider her options. *Maybe we should turn back.* However, since they still had a couple of days' supply of food and water, she decided to continue toward the Mescalero village. Taking note of the sun's position in the sky, she turned and spotted a knoll on the northern horizon, and they set out again.

By afternoon of the third day, they had exhausted their water supply. The men cleared away the thick, pulpy leaves and flesh-tearing spikes of mescal plants, and the women dug out the bulbous white roots to gnaw on. The roots' syrupy dampness barely moist-ened their throats.

The fourth sun after crossing the Rio Grande, they desperately needed water. No one defied Thunder when she announced they had to walk to preserve the horses' strength. Later, Victoria lagged behind, then stumbled and fell. Thunder arrived just as Maria helped her back to her feet.

"Perdón, Señorita Thunder," Victoria said humbly between gasps.

"My mother had a breathing illness years ago," Maria added, "and she does not have the breath to walk very far in this heat."

Thunder thought for a moment, then brought Stormy to them. "Maria, I will leave you to provide for your mother's welfare. She can ride Stormy first, but make sure she changes horses regularly. If there is any problem, tell me at once."

On they walked. Star offered words of encouragement to Thunder whenever possible. She knew very well their lives now depended on one another. They continued on foot, with only the sap of a few milkweeds to sustain them.

Toward nightfall, they came upon what looked like an old buffalo wallow, a few puddles of water fouled with green scum. It looked terrible and smelled worse. Star shook her head in answer to Thunder's silent question. "I will not drink that."

Thunder stepped over to a patch of reeds growing near the water, pulled out her knife, and cut off a bunch. She handed a reed to each person, then cut off the other end of her own. Crouching by the wallow, she inserted the reed through the floating scum and drank. The first swallow refused to stay down, but she had less difficulty with the second.

Eventually, they all drank as much of the rank water as they could stomach. Then, they sucked up more mouthfuls of water and expelled them into their canteens. Thunder let the horses drink what remained of the muddy slime. Judging from the animals' dry, hot skin, the horses needed water even more desperately than they did.

In the next day's evening gloom, a sweltering wind howled across the barren sand hills.

"Let us rest here until the moon rises," Thunder said. Looking grateful, the others dropped their packs and fell to the ground. The blazing sun had blistered their skin, swelling their eyes almost shut.

Stormy led the other horses to a sparse growth of stunted mesquite trees, where they nibbled the sun-dried leaves. The people, however, were too thirsty to have an appetite.

Thunder slept fitfully. Star woke her at moonrise. "You tossed and turned and cried out in your sleep. Are you troubled, sister?"

Thunder buried her face in her hands, and a low, miserable groan escaped her blistered lips. "Yes, I am an unworthy *nantan*. I am afraid I have led us all to our deaths."

"For all things, there is a purpose, sister."

Enraged, Thunder sprang to her feet. "For all of us to die of thirst in the desert? What possible purpose could there be?" Her parched tongue cracked open and started bleeding. The taste of her own blood, another omen—*We are doomed.*

Star took in a long, slow breath. "We traveled into this desert knowing it would be dangerous and we might die. Suffering can harden your heart, or you can use it to bring yourself closer to the spirit world. It is your choice."

Thunder walked into the desert alone, contemplating Star's words. She would shame the spirit of Gray Fox if she gave up. She had to go on living. As long as she carried his memory, he would live through her. She needed to keep him and his wisdom alive in her heart. *You do not always need to understand,* Gray Fox had taught her, *just continue to believe.* She danced on the hot sand, calling his spirit to her. "I am lost, Grandfather. Please give me strength to find the way!" A memory came to her, when she told Grandfather she had not taken a drink the day of her long run. *The only time he chuckled. Odd...He must have known a time would come when I would be much thirstier than that. Now is my real test.* She felt a comforting sense that her grandfather was with her, ready to help. Liberated from doubt, she returned to her companions.

"We must walk again," she declared. "The horses are not strong enough to carry all of us."

The others struggled to their feet.

As they trudged on in the moonlight, Star forgot about her bundle, Thunder lost her need for vengeance, Victoria and Maria no longer valued their freedom, and the Mescaleros did not think of home.

Water was the only thing on their minds.

Turn the pages to start *Singing Wind* and follow the band's plight.

Scan the QR code to dive into book three: *Singing Wind.*

SINGING WIND

Oh, Great spirit
whose voice I hear in the winds,
and whose breath gives life to all the world,
hear me, I am small and weak,
I need your strength and wisdom.

Let me walk in beauty and make my eyes ever
behold the red and purple sunset.
Make my hands respect the things you have made
and my ears sharp to hear your voice.

Make me wise so that I may understand
the things you have taught my people.
Let me learn the lessons you have hidden
in every leaf and rock.

I seek strength, not to be superior to my brother,
but to fight my greatest enemy—myself.
Make me always ready to come to you
with clean hands and straight eyes,
so when life fades, as the fading sunset,
my spirit will come to you without shame.

Lakota Sioux Chief Yellow Lark

ONE

Southwestern Dakota Territory, August 1879

After rising at dawn in her small Sioux village, Singing Wind saw the warriors ride off on another morning hunt.

The sun, a fiery veil of crimson, lit fluffy white clouds drifting lazily across the huge expanse of blue sky. The morning breeze held a pungent mixture of dogwood and paintbrush. Singing Wind thanked the Great Spirit for such a beautiful day.

Kneeling by the stream beside the village, she was washing her mother's doeskin dress when the camp dogs began to yip. Raising her hand to block the sun's glare, Singing Wind saw three braves on foot, naked to the waist, running among the tipis. More men formed a loose circle around the village. Women and children ran crazily about, screaming.

A raid! Run! Cross the stream and hide deep in the briars!

Suddenly, strong arms encircled Singing Wind's abdomen, lifting her off the ground. The man's wild war cries nearly deafened her. She dropped the dress, twisted her agile young body, and repeatedly kicked her heels up into her captor's groin. One kick hit its target, and the warrior bellowed and loosened his grip. As she wrenched herself loose, her heart skipped a beat when she recognized the war paint of a Pawnee.

Sprinting away from the man, Singing Wind saw her mother step out of the tipi and look around, bewildered. "Run, Mother!" she screamed frantically. Her mother met her gaze and began to scurry toward her, but a group of Pawnee warriors blocked her mother from view.

Women and children scrambled out of the village, some crossing the creek, others running into the scrub-filled countryside. The sky swarmed with arrows and swinging war clubs. Dodging several Pawnee warriors, she tried desperately to find her mother amid the mayhem. At last, Singing Wind saw her crumpled on the ground, blood dripping from her head, her eyes open and lifeless.

"Mother!" she screamed. Pawnee warriors were everywhere, like wild dogs scattering a herd of defenseless sheep.

A powerful arm encircled Singing Wind's torso, and she blocked the other arm, causing it to slide over her shoulder. When fingers brushed across her mouth, she caught the index finger between her teeth and bit down with all her might. Her captor let out a bloodcurdling howl. Struggling against his bulk, she tried to free herself again. He smashed his fist into the pit of her stomach, sending a cramping pain throughout her abdomen. She fell to the ground, gasping for air.

The captor yipped shrilly, then bound Singing Wind's wrists

together. Following the other Pawnee, he dragged her from the village to where the few remaining Sioux horses were tied. He grabbed a bridle lying nearby and deftly slipped it on a horse. After mounting, he pulled her up by her arms, set her in front of him, and rode off.

The sun had grown hot by the time the Pawnee warriors reached an isolated sycamore grove. Singing Wind heard soft nickering through the dense growth. When they came closer, she saw her friends Blue Snow and Blackberry on horseback with their hands tied as well. More Pawnee and horses stood in the cool shade.

Without a word, the warriors dismounted, loosed the pack animals, and led their prisoners into a clearing. They brought forth the bounty from the raid: pots, tools, and valuable jewelry.

As Singing Wind's captor untied the straps around her wrists, she studied him closely. The man's blotchy upper lip only covered part of his long, broken, yellowish teeth, which smelled like something rotten. Saying nothing, he pulled her from the horse and threw her belly-down on a worn-looking mule. The thought of her own death caused her to stay very still while he tied her hands and feet under the mule's ribs. The thin rawhide dug deeply into her wrists and ankles, and she gritted her teeth to keep from crying out. She knew not to make trouble, or the Pawnee would kill her as casually as one might squash a brown beetle.

She recalled many stories about the Pawnee and their brutality. Her great aunt had once seen a warrior bash a baby's head in because it was crying. Just thinking about it caused a chill to pass through her body. Her great aunt had been lucky: her husband, their chief, had paid a large ransom to get her back. Singing Wind knew not to expect such good fortune. With her mother dead, she had no family left.

She watched her captor through the narrow slits of her eyes. The warrior embodied everything she had heard about the cold-blooded Pawnee. In her thirteen winters, she had never before seen such a detestable man. The name "Cruel One" stuck in her mind.

After distributing their loot, the Pawnee mounted up again and rode south. The unrelenting pounding of the mule's hooves against the dry, hard earth bounced Singing Wind's abdomen against its back, wrenching her insides in pain. No mortal could be expected to ride at this pace for so long. Yet across the sweltering plains they rode, alternating between a fast walk and a stomach-jolting trot.

Just after sundown, a brilliant moon rose over the hills, spilling its light across the vast grassland. The rippling grass shimmered like silvery waves of water. Nighthawks swooped across the moon's face like moths over a fire, and wolves called their cries of despair to one another. Singing Wind's flesh crawled at the lonely, wailing sound.

The warriors rode south into the deepening night until the moon stood nearly overhead. Eventually, the leader left the trail and walked his horse through a stand of huge oak trees. The rest followed in single file, threading their way through the timber, dodging low-hanging limbs and waist-high briars.

The wolves' eerie howls grew louder as they moved deeper into the woods. Soon, Singing Wind began to see many shadowy shapes. Tipis stood just beyond a makeshift corral holding hundreds of horses. The howling, she realized, had not been wolves. It had come from the Pawnee scouts that must have been riding ahead of them and stopped at this place.

Cruel One halted, slid from his horse, and walked stiff-legged to join a group of men sprawled around the central campfire. After a short conversation, two men staggered over to Singing Wind and dug their fingers into her wrists and ankles. They unfastened the rough leather straps and flung her legs up, somersaulting her into the air. Her rear slammed against the unforgiving ground, and she bit her lip to keep silent. The braves pulled her arms and legs behind her and retied her aching wrists and ankles once again. She struggled like an upside-down water bug that could not right itself.

The Pawnees' loud laughter echoed in the darkness.

She rocked from side to side until her body flopped to rest on her shoulder and hip. From her new position, she saw many Pawnees seated around a fire.

Halfway through the night, the Pawnee warriors stopped drinking and dragged Blue Snow and Blackberry into the fire-lit circle. Their skin and shredded garments showed marks from beatings. A moment later, when two drunken men came to her, Singing Wind screamed in terror. They grabbed her by her tied arms and legs and swung her into a tree. Her head slammed against the hard trunk, and she lost consciousness.

Floating in and out of dreams, she heard someone killing buffalo. From the cries of pain, she concluded they were doing a poor job of it. Helpless and in too much pain to care, she fell back asleep.

When the tortured cries sounded again, Singing Wind's eyes flew open. She moved her head slightly to seek the source of the noise, and her dream world faded instantly. It was not dying buffalo she had heard, but Blue Snow and Blackberry, stripped naked and bound to stakes in the ground. The girls jerked and twitched as the men on top of them thrust themselves deeper into their torn bodies.

Ignoring the girls' pitiful screams, the other men sat joking and laughing as they waited their turns. Horrified, Singing Wind willed her spirit back into the comforting world of darkness.

She awoke to warm liquid splashing on her face, then recognized the acrid smell of urine. Looking up, she saw a drunken man shake off the last drops before shuffling away. She whipped her head around repeatedly to fling off the stench. Blocking out the pain of her cramping muscles and the disgusting odor, she breathed deeply and slowly. After some time, she fell asleep.

At dawn, the dig of a sharp object into her chest wrenched her back to consciousness. The drunken brave prodded her once more, and she smelled the putrid odor of blood and death tainting the morning air. Still, Singing Wind felt lucky to be alive. She thanked Great Spirit that the Pawnee had not violated her as they had her friends.

Cruel One sauntered over, untied the rawhide binding her ankles, then jerked her bound wrists hard. Upward she came, with sharp pain shooting through every muscle in her body.

Cruel One pulled her past Blue Snow and Blackberry, both dead and lying in blood, their throats slit. Singing Wind cringed in horror. His eyes shot a warning that if she didn't obey, she would meet the same fate. The other warriors, already on their horses, waited. Cruel One tied her belly-down onto the mule again, and they resumed their journey.

Throughout the morning, Singing Wind strained repeatedly to catch a glimpse of Cruel One's back. She kept her spirit alive by thinking how good it would feel to plunge a knife between his sagging shoulders. She yearned to see his blood spurting, to watch him topple face down into the dirt. Hatred kept her strong enough to endure.

At midday, her mule started limping. When Cruel One looked back and saw the animal lagging behind, he barked an order and the group stopped. With a twisted smile on his face, he pulled out his knife and cut the straps from her wrists and ankles. Singing Wind slid down from the animal and rubbed her wrists. He gave her a cup of water and a handful of dried meat. It was the first food she'd had in two suns. She hid her hatred of him behind a forced smile.

To her dismay, Cruel One removed her mule's halter and drove the animal away with a slap on the buttocks. While walking to Singing Wind, he cut the halter from the lead rope, then knotted it around her neck. After he mounted his gelding, a swift yank on her leash told her she now had to walk. She jolted forward, lights exploding behind her eyes.

Singing Wind recalled her great aunt's stories about the Pawnee. They believed they obtained their sacred power from the god Morning Star. Having provided the first woman to men, that god periodically required them to sacrifice a young virgin in return. Acceding to Morning Star's demand would ensure renewal of life and prevent the earth's destruction by the fire of the sun.

The Pawnee must have chosen me for their next virgin sacrifice. That is why Cruel One gave me food and water: he wanted to be sure I survived the journey. They did not violate me because they want to sacrifice me to the Pawnee god!

Singing Wind tried to recollect what else her great aunt had said about the sacrifice. All she remembered, however, involved the Pawnee placing the girl on a scaffold and shooting her through the heart. She supposed even that would be better than to die the way Blue Snow and Blackberry had. *No! I must find a way to escape!* Against armed warriors on horses, though, it seemed impossible.

On she walked. By early afternoon the heat had grown unbearable and she needed water, but she dared not ask out of terror that Cruel One would notice her stumbling. If she showed weakness, it would provoke him into treating her even more viciously. She forced herself to concentrate on the gently rolling hills and their array of beautiful colors.

As the sun grew even hotter, Singing Wind grew weaker. Facing the dry, ever-blowing wind parched her throat. The intense heat seemed to lull the small group into silence.

A shrill bird's call brought everyone's attention to the warrior who had made it. He pointed to a dark mass on the horizon. *Bluecoats!*

"Ob-be-mah-e-vah," Cruel One snarled at her. He let go of the leash, and she instinctively tumbled behind a bush.

Sounds of whispering floated from nearby bushes. Singing Wind tensed, the thought of escape racing through her mind. She knew it had to be now or never.

It must be now, her spirit told her. *Now, while they cannot shoot without alerting the soldiers.* If Cruel One found her, he would kill her in a mad rage. Nevertheless, she would prefer a quick death over being sacrificed to the hungry Pawnee god.

She coiled the leash in her hand and began to crawl across the hot sand. *Any moment, Cruel One will grab my hair and wrench my head back.* She could almost feel the blade of his knife sliding across her throat.

Singing Wind kept crawling at a daring pace, stopping only briefly to look over her shoulder. To her relief, she saw no one. A dash of hope stirred in the depths of her soul. *Move away from the soldiers and the Pawnee dogs*, her spirit whispered. She continued slithering across the sandy terrain like a gigantic snake, making no sound save the soft rumbling in her breast as she chanted her prayers:

Spirit of an eagle, see me, help me,
Send brother wolf with eyes to see,
Send brother bear to set me free.

Spirit of an eagle, see me, help me,
Send brother tree that I might hide,
Send brother horse for me to ride.

Spirit of an eagle, see me, help me,
Send sister rain to fill my tracks,
Send brother arrow to Pawnee backs.

Spirit of an eagle, hear me,

Spirit of an eagle, help me,

Spirit of an eagle, save me.

Singing Wind's prayers were answered. When the first gunshots erupted, she sprang to her feet and ran for her life.

TWO

New Mexico Territory, August 1879

The land had grown steep and rocky over the last few miles, slowing Sanchez, José, and Paco to a turtle's pace. Sanchez would have stopped if the sun had not already risen because he worried about breaking the fine-boned legs of his two mares. He did not care so much about the mule he rode. It was accustomed to carrying his overweight body.

As the sun grew higher, the land became gentler and finally leveled off. Neat hedgerows began marking off cultivated fields, and a sparkling stream circled lazily through green pastures. In the distance, Sanchez spotted a herd of longhorn cattle grazing contentedly. Then, he caught sight of the fort, swelling from a dot on the horizon into a solid wall of timber.

At the huge wooden gates of the fort, a freckle-faced boy of seven or eight years ran out to them. "Morning, sir. Y'all look plumb tuckered out and so do your horses. If you need water, there's a cistern right over there and a trough for your horses too."

"*Gracias, nene.* Can you tell me where the man in charge lives?" Relieved he had reached the fort and encountered someone helpful, Sanchez looked forward to washing up and finding rest. But there was still business to do, and his own comfort would wait until after he spoke to the officer.

"Sure, Mister. My father's Captain Baker, and he's at home right now." The boy pointed to a well-kept cabin several yards away. "I'll tell him he has visitors." Sanchez watched as the boy ran to the house.

A moment later, the captain walked out, smiling. He greeted the travelers and invited them to have a seat on the front porch. He told the boy to ask his mother to bring the coffee pot and three more cups. The boy went inside, and a moment later, a woman came through the door bearing a laden tray.

"How can I help you gentlemen?" the captain asked as he filled the cups and passed them around the table.

"*Señor* Captain," Sanchez said, "we were returning home from a trading trip when two Indian girls came into our camp." A frown deepened Sanchez's chubby cheeks as he told Baker how the girls had tricked him, then stolen his servants. "They also burned all my trade goods. We were still in the territory riddled with Mescaleros when we met Sergeant Clark. He told us he and his men were looking for the same girls. He promised to bring the girls here, and I hope he'll bring my servants too."

Captain Baker struggled to understand Sanchez's story. "You say the thieves were two Indian girls?"

"*Sí*, but these girls are not average squaws. They're the devil's spawn!"

"When Clark returns with your property and servants, we'll return them to you," the captain said, suppressing the urge to smile. Sanchez's story sounded familiar, very much like Sergeant O'Riley's. He felt sincerely sorry for the merchant's loss, but the situation was not without a touch of humor. He actually found himself hoping Clark would bring the girls in alive. He looked forward to meeting them.

The captain rose early the next morning. As he took his first sip of coffee, he thought of Sergeant Clark. He had taken his men far too close to the dreaded Mescaleros. The captain finished his breakfast and hurried to his office, where he sent his aide to find Barney and Lieutenant Jackson.

Barney stepped into the captain's office minutes later, and the two waited for Jackson. When the lieutenant finally arrived, the captain noticed sleep in his eyes and his wrinkled clothing. *Probably yesterday's uniform.*

"Lieutenant," the captain said, "I'm concerned about Sergeant Clark and his squad. I sent him out to capture the two Indian girls who have caused so much trouble around here. From what I learned from a Mexican trader yesterday, Clark is dangerously close to the Mescalero stronghold. If you follow the Mexican's tracks south, you should find his squad easily. Take over his command and add his men to yours."

"Yes, sir. When would you like me to go?"

"Now. And you'd better watch yourself, Lieutenant. I hear the girls are pretty damned tricky."

Barney spoke up. "Them 'paches is growed up fer war just like them gol-dang Comanches, sir. They been a-fighting somebody off this here land fer hundreds a' years. Best ya be looking south of the border. Them danged redskins done stole so many women they be kin to half the Mexicans between here and Sonora."

The captain laughed. "Thank you, Barney, for that useful information."

"You orta not be laughing at me, sir, or at them Injuns neither. Them 'paches is thick out there, just like skeeters and snakes. All us ol' trappers knows they's the biggest hazard of doin' business in the badlands. An' 'em youngsters you sent out the other day with the sergeant got a lot a learnin' afore they can find an Apache, much less ketch one, sir."

"All right, Lieutenant," said the captain. "Why don't you just take Barney and his superior knowledge on the patrol with you? And issue him a horse. He'd have a hard time keeping up with the rest of you on his burro."

"Yes, sir," the lieutenant said with a smart salute. He hurried down the steps, embarrassed the captain had seen him hungover and still in the clothes he had slept in. He had never drunk so much back East. This godforsaken place was enough to drive any man to drink.

THREE

New Mexico Territory, August 1879

The air thickened and became humid. Hope filled the hearts of Thunder and her followers as they tramped through the night. But with the rising sun, the promise of rain died. Still, the sight of a road elated the footsore travelers. Hardly a real road, it consisted of two narrow strips where wagon wheels had killed the prairie grass.

The haggard group dropped onto the hot, dry earth to rest. After a brief exchange of opinions, everyone agreed it would be wiser to follow the trail. However, they would have to stay on guard for passing wagon trains.

The northeastward path led them into a country of low, rust-colored hills. Yucca dotted the land, and birds began to appear. In the distance, the ground rose higher. Hope soared in their hearts again.

The desert would soon give way to the hills and green valleys of the mountains.

Late morning, as Thunder led the band up a slope, she felt the ground softer under her feet. Many steps later, mud caking to her moccasins brought forth a surge of exhilaration.

"It rained here last night!"

After some time, Stormy threw his head back and whinnied. He galloped into low-lying woodland, followed by the thirsty travelers. Flashes of a glistening river shone between the trees! The group rushed ahead giving it their all—but none could muster more than a half trot. They clumsily made their way to its bank and dropped to their knees. Plunging their heads into the river, they sucked in the fresh, revitalizing water.

Thunder's parched tongue and palate tingled as the water came rushing in. She swallowed rapaciously, the first gulp of cool liquid inching its way down and spilling into her stomach. *Thank you, Great One, for the life-giving water!* Taking swallow after swallow, she finally forced herself to stop. Lifting her head, she took a deep breath and whispered, "Thank you, Grandfather, for guiding us here."

Star sat nearby, flinging her long, wet hair away from her face as the others continued guzzling. "Everybody stop drinking!" Star shouted. Thunder quickly translated her words into Spanish.

Victoria and the Mescaleros slowly raised their faces from the stream. The men stood and walked to the horses. They patted the horses' flanks as they took the ropes from the saddles, slung them around the animals' necks, and pulled them back from the stream. Maria, however, still drank deeply.

Thunder knew Star was right. "Maria, you must stop now!" She ran to her, grabbed her shoulders, and pulled her back from the stream.

Maria yanked Thunder's hair with her left hand and swung to slap her with her right. "Just let me drink!"

Thunder blocked the blow. "You have had enough, Maria!"

"I have not!" Maria yelled, kicking at Thunder. "Leave me alone!"

Thunder peeled Maria's grip from her hair and pushed her to the ground. "If you drink any more, you will get sick and die!"

Maria said nothing. She stared coldly at Thunder, on the verge of fighting her way back to the stream to quench her voracious thirst.

"Maria," Star said, "please fetch the bag of salt *Señor* Coronado gave us." As she spoke, Thunder calmed herself and translated Star's instructions. "Pour half the salt in a cooking bowl and give it to the Mescaleros for the horses. Then, give each of us a handful. We must take in salt as we drink."

Maria slowly stood and walked to the mule. Victoria followed, knowing she would need to calm her daughter. Grateful for Thunder's and Star's concern, she smiled, thinking their knowledge always surprised her.

As Maria pulled the provisions from the pack, Victoria put her hand on her shoulder. "I know you were spellbound at the stream, Maria—I could barely take my mouth from the water too. Only *Señorita* Thunder's concern for your life caused her to pull you away from the river."

"I never thought water could kill me," Maria said as she took out the bag of salt. "My thirst has lessened now. I'll try to let it pass."

By mid-afternoon, they all gradually drank until everyone had their fill. Exhaustion now replacing their thirst, they scattered and prepared to nap in the shade along the river.

Scan the QR code to read *Singing Wind.*

Marjorie Carter was born in Salem, Missouri, on July 17, 1937. Of Cherokee descent, she learned the traditional ways of her relatives from early childhood. During the eight grade, she was forced to leave school to work and provide for her younger brothers. At the age of nineteen, she moved to Texas and began her careers in the restaurant and real estate businesses. During her life, she was diagnosed with seven different cancers and fought against melanoma for 25 years. A Native American seer and shaman, she had a passion for art, poetry, and stories. She wrote at her ranch near San Miguel de Allende, Mexico, hoping that Red With Native Blood would help reservation students embrace their heritage. Marjorie died of pneumonia on July 12, 2004.

Randal Nerhus received a BS in Agricultural Studies from Iowa State University in 1982, and an MA in Oriental Philosophy and Religion from Bananas Hindu University, India, in 1988. Shortly after obtaining his agricultural degree, he volunteered with the Peace Corps in the Philippines. While traveling in the mountains on the island of Palawan, he visited a remote tribal village and encountered a very different way of life—one of community, contentment, happiness, and love. Fifteen years later, his interest in tribal traditions deepened while taking part in a ManKind Project initiation that used native approaches to bring men into a life of integrity. In 2002, Marjorie Carter took him under her shamanic guidance which complemented and expanded on his early Christian foundations. From 2013 to 2016, he lived in Colombia's Amazon jungle studying under Cocama shaman don Rogelio Carihuasari, and relevant parts of that experience were incorporated into the trilogy.

Learn more about the *Red With Native Blood* series, as well as news and events at:

Randalnerhus.com

Facebook: Randal Nerhus-Red With Native Blood

RandalNerhus on Twitter

RandalNerhus on Instagram

Randal Nerhus on LinkedIn

Randal Nerhus on TikTok

Printed in Great Britain
by Amazon

41215928R00108